T0372486

FISHING IN FIRE

FISHING IN FIRE

TRENT REEDY

Norton Young Readers

An Imprint of W. W. Norton & Company
Celebrating a Century of Independent Publishing

For information about permission to reproduce selections from this book, write to
Permissions, W. W. Norton & Company, Inc., 500 Fifth Avenue, New York, NY 10110

For information about special discounts for bulk purchases, please contact
W. W. Norton Special Sales at specialsales@wwnorton.com or 800-233-4830

Manufacturing by Lake Book Manufacturing
Book design by Beth Steidle and Hana Anouk Nakamura
Production manager: Delaney Adams

ISBN 978-1-324-01141-5

W. W. Norton & Company, Inc., 500 Fifth Avenue, New York, N.Y. 10110
www.wwnorton.com

W. W. Norton & Company Ltd., 15 Carlisle Street, London W1D 3BS

1 2 3 4 5 6 7 8 9 0

This book is dedicated to my good friend Khalid Siddiq, one of the bravest and most brilliant men I've ever known.

FISHING IN FIRE

CHAPTER 1

ANNETTE WILLARD LIKED TO COLLECT QUOTATIONS, carefully copying them into a gorgeous leather-bound notebook Mom and Dad had given her last Christmas. She found these in the books she read and on social media posts. Lines such as "To thine own self be true" by William Shakespeare, or "I am the master of my fate. I am the captain of my soul" by poet William Ernest Henley. Online, these words appeared over a simple white square or with a beautiful nature scene in the background. Annette's favorites were the ones about a person writing her own life story or about living the kind of life about which someone would want to write.

Living a good story was Annette's high goal that late August evening. But unlike the rush of excitement and satisfaction she experienced as she closed in on the perfect ending of a story for the *McCall Middle School Times*, Annette faced only worry and doubt. When writing an article, she knew the importance of a good lead line and the who, what, when, where, and why. She knew the correct use of semicolons even though she hated them and would never use one. She understood plenty about writing, but when it came to fashion she was clueless.

She'd borrowed an old blue dress from her sister that showed her shoulders and had a skirt that descended to just above the knee. Janelle had looked great in this dress when she'd worn it to the Snowflake Ball in seventh grade. But athletic and confident Janelle didn't have Annette's frizzy hair, freckles, braces, and mountain of doubts.

"Trust me," Janelle said as she dropped Annette off near the south end of McCall's Lake Payette. Whenever her popular, soon-to-be-senior-in-high-school sister said, *Trust me*, it always sounded like, *I know more than you.* Which, since she was older and probably did, was a fact that made her superior tone no less annoying. "You'll be fine. The dance is no big deal."

"Only because you're not involved and don't care," Annette replied quietly as Janelle drove away.

The end-of-summer, welcome-to-the-new-school-year middle school dance was always held on the Lake Street terrace overlooking the beach and lake. Annette looked at the water sparkling in the light of the remaining evening sun. The last of the day's boats and Jet Skis would be coming in soon. Annette remembered fishing with Dad back before he'd been forced to take the job all the way down in Boise. A lot of summer mornings and evenings, it was just the two of them in their little old fishing boat on the lake or on the Payette River, about the only time she ever had her father all to herself, the only time she had any peace in her large family. Not a small part of her wished she were out on the water now.

But this dance might make a good story for the paper, Annette told herself. She shook her head. No. This wasn't about writing other people's stories. The whole point of tonight was to create some of her own. She took a deep breath and headed onto the terrace, the heat of the day still rising in waves off the concrete against her bare legs.

Her sister had said the evening would mostly consist of boys standing on one side of the dance area and girls on the other. As a fun new hip-hop song echoed through the cool evening air, most people did stand around. But they were further divided due to the war.

Sixth grade had turned into a disaster when the rivalry between the two popular girls Swann Siddiq and McKenzie Crenner broke into a war, and it seemed everybody had been forced to take sides. McKenzie especially wouldn't allow any middle ground. Hunter Higgins and Kelton Fielding stuck with Swann after their snowmobile ordeal, and Annette's best friend Yumi stayed with Hunter. For months, everybody in the sixth grade was caught deep in a web of mean notes, texts, and cruel anonymous social media posts. The school guidance counselor's "Be a Buddy, Not a Bully" campaign hadn't helped at all. And when Annette had written an article in the school paper calling for everybody to get along, for an end to the war, she'd suffered attacks from both sides. Even Yumi had been mad at her about that article. This dance, marking the end of summer and the start of seventh grade, was Annette's effort to leave all that behind and start over.

And if Hunter saw her and actually liked her dress and asked her to dance under the stars, maybe the two of them would start going out. That might help fix things between her and Yumi. And also, it could just be pretty great.

As she approached the dance area, alone, she felt a greater need to join one of the groups. At last she spotted Yumi, standing with Kelton Fielding and Swann Siddiq near the edge of the event. Hunter was on the far side of the dance, chomping on a cookie near the snack table. A few paces away from Hunter, talking to some popular eighth-grade girls, were McKenzie Crenner and her friend Morgan Vaughn.

"Hey, everyone," Annette said as she approached Swann, Yumi, and Kelton.

Swann wore a brilliant floral-pattern summer dress, a little frayed at the bottom, like some kind of 1960s hippie throwback outfit, her black hair up in a cool twist. She pulled Annette into a one-armed hug, looking her over. "Annie!"

Annette forced a smile. She hated being called Annie.

Yumi tugged the bottom of her Fortnite T-shirt and smoothed her hands over her denim skirt. She did not seem as pleased to see Annette as Annette had hoped she would be. Was she still mad about that stupid article?

"Hi, Annette." Kelton, in his tan shorts and slightly wrinkled button shirt, was as dressed up as the guy ever was.

Others had noticed Annette's arrival too. McKenzie Crenner wrinkled her nose, elbowed one of the older girls, and nodded toward Annette before they both giggled.

Maybe it had been a mistake to wear this dress. Maybe everyone could tell it didn't really fit her, or rather, that she didn't really fit the dress. Yumi was dressed pretty casually. Morgan had on tan shorts and a loose blouse. McKenzie sported new jean shorts and a light button-up shirt that showed off her midriff. She looked like a sophisticated clothing model on a beach shoot.

I look more like a little girl who's way too old to still be playing dress-up, Annette thought. *What was I thinking? I'm going to be a joke for everybody all night. I should have stuck to writing other people's stories. That's the only story I'll ever have.*

"How's everything going?" Annette said. "Doesn't seem like many people are dancing."

"Well, I don't know how," Kelton blurted out. "So I'm good just standing here."

"Sorry to tell an at-my-old-school story . . ." Swann held her hands up in apology. Back when she and her famous actor parents lived in Hollywood, Swann had attended a fancy private school. But she'd told Kelton, who'd told Hunter, who'd told Yumi, who'd told Annette, that Swann really wanted to downplay her rich-girl image. "But there were girls and boys there who'd taken a bunch of dance lessons, like hip-hop and who knows what else. I mean, some of their parents had danced professionally in movies and on the stage. Anyway, I went to one school dance in this huge ballroom and some of them just lit it up. I'm serious. It looked choreographed!"

"Like this?" Kelton put his hands up together over his head, spun around, and jumped, kicking out his leg in what Annette assumed to be his impression of a ballet dancer.

"No." Swann laughed. "Please stop!"

Yumi had been eyeing the snack table the whole time. Hunter was over there having a cookie and talking to Mason Bridger. Mason mimed like he was whipping a fishing rod to cast. That was what Mason did. Annette loved fishing. But Mason lived for it.

Annette hadn't talked to Yumi much since the article. Yumi always claimed to be too busy to reply to texts, and when she did, she only quickly answered questions and asked none of her own. Her attitude so far was crushing Annette's hopes that this in-person meeting could help them patch things up.

I told you writing that school news opinion piece was a bad idea, Yumi had said back when Annette's call for peace only brought a wave of snarky attacks down on her. *Let those two fashion-queen popular girls tear each other apart. Don't get involved in the war. Higgins is already too wrapped up in it.*

"I'm going to go talk to Higgins for a sec." Yumi vanished, catching weird glances from McKenzie Crenner's crowd as she moved lightly, almost dancing, across the empty middle of the dance area.

"Why does she call Hunter by his last name if her name is Yumi Higgins?" Swann asked.

Annette was grateful for a reason to laugh and lighten her mood. "I know Yumi better than anyone, and that is one of the biggest mysteries. I asked her once, and she only said, 'Because his last name is Higgins.' Those two are the most best-friend cousins you'll ever meet."

"Must be nice to have all that family," Swann said. "I'm an only child, and my father has one childless brother."

"I'd gladly give you a few of my siblings," Annette said. "My house is always crowded. My brothers fight constantly over the stupidest stuff—toys or who gets the larger piece of the cookie they're sharing. There's basically no place to be alone at my house."

Swann looked at the lake. "I wonder what that's like."

"The worst. I promise," Annette said. The music kept thumping. Some eighth-grade girls laughed as they tried some dance moves while the boys watched. "Hey, Swann. I'm sorry about that article I wrote. I wanted to stop all the arguing and meanness, but I should have known it would only make things worse."

Swann turned her attention back to Annette with her magic model's smile. Annette thought she would never be so pretty herself. "Oh, Annette," Swann said. "I'm sorry if I seemed like I was mad at you. I was more angry with the situation. What did you say in the article that was so terrible? Nothing! You were right that the whole war is stupid. McKenzie was seriously mad when I showed up to school wearing a different brand of jeans? She's the clothes police now?"

Annette considered mentioning that Swann was pointing out the stupidity of the war by practically launching a fresh attack, but Swann seemed friendly to her, at least, and friends had been in short supply lately.

Swann must have realized what she was doing as well, because she suddenly clapped a hand over her own mouth and was quiet for a moment. "No. I'm not getting into all that again. Your article was absolutely right, and you were very brave to write it. Back in L.A., the girls at my old school—" She stopped herself. "It's not important. I'm *here* now. Let's . . . dance."

To the sweets, give me sugar, hit the lights up till you drop. It was a fast song by a new K-pop group, one of those catchy melodies that would be stuck in her head all night. *I'm your hero, I'm your baby, and our love will never stop.*

"Oh, I don't know anything about dancing to this kind of—"

"Neither do I!" Swann took her by the hand and started a quick hop-step-and-wavy-arms kind of move.

Annette tried to match her, but felt, as she always did in dancing or sports, that her arms and legs never seemed to do what she wanted them to do, like her body was an awkward over-long assembly of loose spaghetti. "I feel so stupid."

"Then you must be doing something right," Swann answered.

"Everybody will make fun of me. Hashtag: Annette-Can'tDance."

"Maybe," said Swann. "But we've both seen worse."

"I feel like I'm flopping around like a fish out of water," Annette said.

"My father and I have been fishing," Swann said. "Good way to spend time together and leave the internet behind, you know? It's just too bad we're terrible at fishing."

"I love fishing," Annette said with a smile, though the simple statement didn't fully express the wonder of the sport in her life.

"Maybe we could go together sometime?" Swann said.

Swann had moved here to McCall a year ago, but Annette still wasn't quite used to someone with her famous background asking about such a normal thing as fishing.

"Sounds great," Annette said.

The song ended, and after a tiny pause, a slow song came on.

The snow is coooold. Our love will hoooold on.

Unfreeze my heart! Unfreeeeeeeze my heeeaaaart!

"Oh, I hate this song," said Swann. "I actually met this singer, Adia, at the *Snowtastrophe III* premier screening. Complained constantly about her seat, and the quality of the refreshments, and everything. Cold as ice, until the cameras were on her."

"Unfreeze My Heart," the love theme from Swann's father's hit movie *Snowtastrophe III*, had been a top ten hit all summer. There were parodies and up-tempo dance remixes all over YouTube, but this original, super-romantic version echoed across the pavement and lake now. Annette craned her neck, looking for Hunter, while trying to avoid being too obvious in looking for Hunter. He was still at the snack table. How many cookies could the guy eat? Had he glanced in her direction? Was he coming to ask her to dance?

Kelton Fielding slid to Swann's side. "Um, hey." His cheeks were flaming red. He took a deep breath. "Would you like to, you know? Dance?"

Swann's scowl melted, and she touched his cheek. "Oh, Kel. Only you could make this song bearable." She smiled, and the two of them moved to an open space to dance.

Yumi returned to Annette, arms folded. She looked as uncomfortable as Annette felt. She nodded toward Swann and Kelton. "Are those two, like, together?"

Annette shrugged. Yumi'd been basically ignoring her since she got here, and only wanted to talk now that Swann and Kelton were dancing? What was her problem?

"I'm an aspiring journalist, not a gossip columnist."

"Right," Yumi said.

Annette looked to Hunter again. He ran his hand back through his hair, like one of those cute boys on a cheesy teen movie. Was he doing that on purpose? Did he know she was watching him? Annette wasn't sure which was more awkward, waiting in that stupid dress with nobody to dance with, or standing next to Yumi and the two of them not talking.

"Hey, Yumi?" Mason Bridger materialized from the crowd, looking almost as nervous as Kelton had been a moment ago. "Would you like to dance?"

Yumi silently stared at him for a long uncomfortable moment.

And with a billion snowflakes floating down, there's just only one of you.

You unfreeze my heart, and now my love is shining through!

"Yes," Yumi said quietly, and, appearing stunned, took his outstretched hand in her own, following his lead to the middle of the dance area.

There were a lot of couples dancing now, and some of them, especially the ones who had been dating for a while, swayed together kind of close. Maybe she should have just asked Hunter to dance. But the song was almost half over. There'd be another. Maybe he'd ask her then. She wasn't a loser for being left out of one dance. It would all go better with the next slow song.

But Hunter didn't ask her to dance with the next slow song. He was in the bathroom for the third slow song.

More people were getting into the dance, overcoming their shyness and moving more. And here she was, wearing her sister's way-too-fancy dress, realizing she'd been hoping for a triumphant Cinderella situation but was more suited to the role of the overworked and cast-aside sister.

Swann danced with Kelton once more, and then accepted an invitation from someone else. Yumi treated the Mason Bridger situation like no big deal until he asked her to dance again. Then she just seemed confused.

Later that night, when Adia's other big romantic hit started to play, Annette took a deep breath. *You're being stupid*, she told herself. *He's your friend, at least. Just go talk to him. Ask him to . . .*

Morgan Vaughn stepped up to Hunter with her big beautiful popular smile. She said something. He nodded. She giggled. Then the two of them were dancing. And what was her problem? She pulled him in almost boyfriend-girlfriend close.

"No way," Yumi said quietly, resuming her place at Annette's side. "After what she posted in the spring about Hunter?"

"We don't know that she wrote that—"

"That was her," Yumi snapped.

When the song ended, a woman at the DJ table spoke over a microphone. "Thanks so much for joining us for the welcome-back dance. You were all great tonight, and we wish you the very best in the coming school year."

Annette watched helplessly as Morgan and Hunter remained close, even after the song was over and floodlights switched on. That was it. All for nothing. She'd lost her chance.

Swann and Kelton joined them. "That was fun," Swann said. "Wasn't it fun?"

Kelton smiled at her in the strangest way. "Totally fun."

"It was . . . interesting," Yumi said.

The dance had not been fun. It hadn't even been simply boring. It had been horrible. Just once, Annette had hoped to be, not the star maybe, but appreciated as more than the smart responsible girl, a babysitter at home, and homework help at school. Annette saw her sister park on the street to pick her up.

"Well, I'll see you," she said to the others. Hunter had joined their little circle, and Annette could hardly look at him.

"Well, hang on," Swann said. "Summer isn't over. We aren't just going home to wait for school, are we?"

Annette watched her, this amazingly beautiful and sophisticated newcomer who had no worries, no doubts. Why couldn't Annette figure out how to be even a little bit like Swann? She stared into the darkness of Payette Lake. Why couldn't life be as simple and honest as fishing?

"Let's go fishing," Annette said without thinking. "Tomorrow." She looked at the rest of her group. Swann's smile showed she was in. Kelton looked excited too.

"Let's get out of here. Someplace by ourselves. You have fishing poles?" They all nodded. "Great! I'll bring the tackle. I know some great fishing spots. How about Painted Pond? Hunter? Yumi? What do you think?" The dance might have been a disaster, but she knew about fishing. She wouldn't be so clueless by the water, reeling in fish. And it would be a much better chance to figure things out with Yumi. And maybe even with Hunter.

"Bit of a hike, but yeah," Yumi said.

"Painted Pond?" Swann asked.

"I've heard of it, but never been there," said Kelton.

"It's a great place," Annette said. "You'll see." Annette told them about how she and her dad used to fish there a lot. All of them, Hunter included, agreed to meet the next morning to begin the trip deep into the woods to the pond. She felt something like the confidence and optimism she'd had earlier that evening returning. The dance hadn't been a total loss. It had offered Annette this one extra chance to fix things with her friends, and to finally make a good story of her own.

CHAPTER 2

"GABE. GABE, DID YOU HEAR WHAT I SAID?" ANNETTE ASKED nervously. "Gabe?"

"Huh? Yeah, Annie, just wait a sec, OK?" Gabe never took his eyes off the TV screen as he tapped away at his controller, his player in the game mowing down terrorists with a machine gun. "Food or something? No problem. Just let me finish this part. I gotta reach the end of this street before time's up and the bomb goes off."

"Sandwiches, Gabe. I made you and Dakota sandwiches." She checked her phone. Already seven-thirty. "Ham and cheese for you. Peanut butter and jelly for Dakota. They're in the fridge. Chips in the pantry."

"You leaving, Annie?" Dakota was coming down the stairs, flying two new Lego spaceship robot things in his hands. That kid could play with his Legos for hours unless Gabe barged in to bother him. Why did he have to emerge right now, today of all days?

"Just going fishing."

Dakota pointed at the screen. "Gabe, grab that sniper rifle up on the ledge." To Annette he added, "But Mom said you're supposed to be watching us."

"Mom said it was fine if I went fishing," Annette said. It wasn't a lie. Mom had said it was OK if Annette went fishing with her friends *sometime*. Now was sometime.

"Sniper rifle?" said Gabe. "Dakota, you're probably the worst gamer of all time."

"Shut up! I am not! Just because you made it farther on *Call of Duty*."

Annette watched the two of them, hypnotized by the game and absorbed in arguing with each other. With Janelle at work, and Kyle sleeping before his afternoon ninth-grade football practice, she was supposed to babysit the younger two. But they didn't need her. Like the rest of the family, they mostly ignored her. Without another word, Annette slipped on her backpack and grabbed her tackle box and best fishing pole. Then she took the little key from the hook by the back door, before hurrying out across their crunchy dry lawn to the shed beside the garage.

The family's John Deere Gator was fully gassed up and ready to go. As ATVs went, the Gator was far from the coolest. Some McCall people liked to drive wicked-fast and rugged outdoor vehicles like the Honda Talon around trails through the wilderness. She'd seen awesome four-wheelers in the Higgins family hunting lodge. The John Deere Gator, Dad had assured Mom, with its little cargo box in back, was for hauling dirt or rocks for his unending gardening efforts or for transporting lumber, tools, and other construction supplies for his ongoing house remodel project. The bright green beast could fight through deep snow or thick mud and haul up to five hundred pounds, but its top speed was less than thirty. It had four seats, enough to fit her and all of her friends if people squeezed together in the back.

Annette, at nearly thirteen years of age, had two issues with the Gator. Driving it on roads and trails required both for her to wear a helmet—*No problem*, she thought, slipping hers on—and the supervision of a licensed adult operator. It was *mostly* legal for her to be driving this vehicle.

"I've been trapped at home all summer," she said to herself, dropping enough helmets for everyone else in the Gator's cargo space. "This is the first and only chance I've had to be with people my age." It was the best opportunity for fun since the start of the war. She turned the key and the machine fired up. "This is mostly legal.

"Life isn't a story to think about and revise forever," Annette said. "Sometimes you just have to go for it." She shifted into forward high and rolled clear of the shed and down the driveway out onto the road.

About ten minutes later, she arrived at the agreed-upon meeting place, a small clearing off Eastside Drive overlooking Lake Payette. Swann, Yumi, Kelton, and Hunter waited with their assortment of backpacks and fishing poles, having been dropped off by their parents who thought they'd be fishing right there.

She brought the Gator to a halt, pulled off her helmet, and shook out her always-too-puffy hair. Kelton smiled and elbowed Hunter, who frowned and pushed Kelton away. *What was that about?*

"Wow," Yumi said as she examined the Gator. "Miss Perfect, you really did it." Was Yumi saying that because she was impressed by Annette's boldness in borrowing the Gator, or was she making fun of her? It was hard to tell.

Hunter and Kelton laughed.

"Gutsy, Annette," Hunter said.

"I don't get it," Swann said. "What did she do?"

Yumi rolled her eyes, but sounded playful when she answered. "Listen, Hollywood. Maybe you didn't know this—"

"I live here now," Swann said evenly.

"I don't know how they do things in California, but here in Idaho a kid without a driver's license isn't allowed to drive one of these things off her property unless an adult's around."

"I did not know that," Swann admitted. "Is it weird that it kind of makes all of this even more exciting?"

Annette wished, not for the first time, that she was capable of taking a compliment, especially one from a cool person, without her cheeks flaring red and hot.

"I brought enough helmets for everybody else," Annette said. "Sorry. Some of them belong to my brothers and probably smell gross."

"Well, let's get going while the morning's still a little cool." Yumi put her fishing pole in the Gator's back cargo space and, holding on to her CamelBak pack and thermos, swung into the passenger seat beside Annette. Everyone followed her lead in loading their gear.

"You know," Kelton said after he, Hunter, and Swann had squeezed into the two backseats, "we could just fish right here, like we told our parents. Catch some sweet trout."

"If we wanted to hang out with the rest of the tourists who are probably searching for Sharlie the lake monster, yeah," Yumi said.

"I want to see this Painted Pond," Swann said. "I've heard about it. A high school party place?"

"Yeah," Annette said. "But no parties this early in the morning. My dad and I used to fish there sometimes. We can take the Gator most of the way there on this rough trail."

They all slipped on their helmets and set off. The Gator's engine ran kind of loud, and in their helmets they couldn't hear well, so the group settled into silence as Annette drove down the road and then off onto the trail. She might have been unable to stop the war, but so far this little fishing trip seemed like it was reuniting at least one faction in the struggle, and soon they'd all be well outside of phone coverage area, safe from any mean online comments.

Annette hit a bump, launching the Gator and everyone in it up in the air a little. Lucky thing it had good shocks. After the vehicle smacked back down, she was about to apologize, but everybody clapped and cheered, like her mistake was a big, cool, deliberate stunt. She pumped her fist in the air like a champion off-road race driver, or, as she knew nothing about off-road race driving—was that even a thing?—the way she imagined such a pro would do it.

Eventually the Gator had taken them as far as it could. It was good at driving off-road, but the trail disintegrated ahead and they had to cross a wide rocky expanse crowded with trees and shrubs. She and Dad had tried to drive through there once but ended up spending over an hour working to get the little vehicle unstuck. They all dismounted, removed their helmets, and grabbed their gear.

Swann leaned forward, holding out her phone to get the perfect shot of the way ahead. She looked half jungle commando and half outdoor clothing website model, wearing a cute little olive-drab military-style backpack, expensive hiking boots, tan cargo shorts, a black T-shirt, and a cool green Army-style vest with many pockets, the kind that looked old and a little worn, but came like that new from the store. Annette often sported old, worn outfits too, but they were mostly pieces Janelle had once enjoyed new.

How did girls like Swann, McKenzie, and Morgan always know how to look so great, without even seeming to try? Annette thought for a moment about her cut-off jean shorts and old TAKE A HIKE T-shirt. Her sagging plain maroon school backpack. Only her fishing pole was worth anything, a legacy of the semi-serious fishing phase she and Dad had enjoyed together.

"How far do we have to go?" Swann asked.

Annette smiled, taking some encouragement from being the

expert and leader here. "Only a couple of miles." There was really no trail, but through the trees she could see the big whitish rock face that rose high on one side of the pond.

Hunter broke a long slender white stick from a nearby aspen tree, swung it twice like a sword, and then tapped one end on the ground, his walking stick ready. "Awesome. Let's go."

"We should have done this, like, weeks ago," Swann said. "Why haven't we been hiking and stuff all summer? Just trooping off into the middle of nowhere to do some fishing together."

"You know, Swann," said Yumi lightly, "this isn't like a documentary that you need to narrate."

"OK, grumpy." Swann laughed a little. "Maybe you'll cheer up with one of the cans of Coke in my backpack. Plus, I have a Snickers bar for each of us. And a little ice pack so they won't melt."

"I'm good. I brought a thermos of coffee," Yumi said.

"I brought a pack of beef jerky," said Kelton.

"When did you start drinking coffee, Yumi?" Annette asked. "You're twelve, not forty-four."

"Sometimes my dad and I go for morning hikes," Yumi said. "We never go without coffee."

Annette was happy to hear Yumi and her father were getting along so well. That hadn't always been the case.

"Hot coffee?" Kelton asked. "On a hot summer day like this?"

"Well, the day's not hot yet, is it?" Yumi fired back.

The morning was perfect. Normally the grass and low shrubbery would have been dew-soaked at this hour, but rain hadn't fallen in weeks. The low rising sun shone in dusty beams of light through the pines. The gentle breeze shook the little round aspen leaves, darker on top than at the bottom, so that they seemed to sparkle in dazzling ripples.

As they walked through the shadows in the cool morning, Annette took in a deep satisfied breath, marveling at this outdoor cathedral that reached for miles. She grew quiet as a still spirit of reverence came over her.

On the far side of the rocky expanse, they reached a section of rising rock. They were getting closer. A little gurgling creek cascaded in a small waterfall down the dark basalt cliff. Amazing. *Anything is possible,* she thought, *out here in the wilderness with these people.*

Hunter stopped and pointed at some poop with his walking stick. "Deer," he said, lifting the stick to his shoulder and scanning the woods as though he held a rifle. Annette smiled. Hunter was such a great shooter.

"A deer's been here," said Swann. "Automatically your first instinct is to shoot it?"

"Well, not out of season," said Hunter.

"And not with a stick," Kelton added.

Hunter and Kelton laughed.

It was neat to see how they'd become friends after their snowmobile adventure.

Swann bumped Kelton with her shoulder, pushing him a little. He didn't resist much. Yumi caught Annette's eye like, *What's going on with these two?*

"I'd love to go hunting with you sometime," Swann said. "Or maybe we could all go?"

"Sure," Hunter said doubtfully. "Well, there's a safety class you have to take. And you need a license. And—"

"And take it from me," Annette said, "the Higgins family is super-intense about hunting. They take it very seriously."

"Right, so could we get going before it gets super-hot?" Yumi motioned down the trail.

"It is amazing out here," Swann said after they'd resumed walking for a few minutes. "I mean, California has plenty of beautiful views too. But a lot of it's super-developed. Like, yeah, the ocean is gorgeous, but it's also full of surfers or else there's a container ship out there. Before moving to Idaho, I never knew wilderness like this still existed in America outside national parks like Yosemite.

"It is beautiful. The mountains. The cliffs. All the trees." Kelton stepped up beside Swann. "And no snow. No freezing deadly avalanches." Kelton's hand moved close to hers and their fingers intertwined for a moment.

"So are you two dating, or what?" Yumi almost shouted.

Kelton fell back a step behind Swann. "What?"

"You heard me," Yumi said. "Pretty sure what I said is still echoing through the valley. Are. You. And. Swann. Dating?"

"Well, you know . . ." Kelton shoved his hands in the pockets of his jeans. He glanced at Swann but wouldn't look at anyone else. "It's . . . who's to say what . . . like, have we gone out, like on a date to the movies, or do you mean . . ."

Swann's cheeks were about as red as Kelton's. She took his hand and turned back to face Yumi. "Kind of. Yes."

Her *yes* seemed to have flipped a switch in Kelton, because his nervousness vanished, replaced by the warmest, most excited smile. "Yes," Kelton said. "We're dating."

Swann moved closer to him so they walked hand in hand and shoulder to shoulder. "Who would have thought a SuperPop and a Grit could be together?" she said. The two of them smiled and looked at each other for a long moment.

"Well, that's great, you two," Hunter said. Hunter glanced Annette's way for a moment, but then turned back toward the woods. Or had she imagined it? Annette walked a little faster. "There." She pointed. "Just coming into view around the bend. See it?"

A high rock ridge rose up before them, with a steep thirty-foot-tall cliff cut into its side. The lower part of the cliff was completely covered with spray paint. Semi-detailed murals were intermixed with crude stick-figure drawings and tons of writing. Political messages. Obscenities. As they approached, they could make out more details.

A bunch of logs had been moved down by the nearby pond, used to hold in looser, smoother dirt and sand, forming a crude beach with a stone circle firepit on it.

"My sister says high school kids come here to party sometimes," Annette explained. "But the pond is fed by a steady stream, and it's clear and deep. The perfect place to cast for some trout."

"It's a . . . spray-paint graffiti-covered cliff?" Swann asked. "We had stuff like this back in L.A."

"Listen, California—" Yumi started.

"Stop!" Annette hissed. "What's that sound?"

Laughter echoed from behind a cluster of boulders by the water. A playful scream, and more laughter.

"High school party?" Kelton whispered.

McKenzie, Morgan, and Mason emerged from behind the rocks.

"Of course." Yumi sighed. "Just great."

A RUSTY TOYOTA COROLLA SPED AROUND A CURVE UP EASTSIDE
Drive, its nearly bald tires squealing a little. Smoke puffed from the driver's-side window. Inside, a middle-age man cursed under his breath and took another long drag on the stub of his cigarette. His foreman at the mill had just told him he was laid off again, which was crap, because he'd been about ready to fork over a down payment for a newer, more reliable used car. Now he was stuck with this old wreck with its odometer stuck at 146,000 miles, reverse gear sometimes not working, and a touchy battery that made it a real rough gamble as to whether or not the car would actually start.

The man leaned over to open the glove box. Napkins. The stupid car manual. A knife. Packet of ketchup. He cursed again, sure that he had at least half a pack of cigarettes somewhere in there. Cigarette smoke wafted up in his eye and he blinked against the sting, the car swerving a little for a moment.

He flicked the end of his cigarette out the window. The light white papery thing whipped in the wind, flipping end over end until it fell to the rough pavement, a few red-hot ashes sparking off it. There it lay, resting in a tiny sandy crack as the loud mufflerless Toyota ground its way down the road until finally its rough engine roar faded away in the distance and all was quiet, save for the whisper of the breeze through the needles of the ponderosa pines. The cigarette shook a little in the light wind, a tiny trail of smoke rising from its fading ember. A black ant approached the object in its path, antennae inspecting the obstacle. Then the wind picked up and shook the cigarette out of the crack and away from the ant, rolling and bumping across the pavement and the sandy shoulder until it came to rest in a bed of dry brown pine needles.

The heat faded from the cigarette so that its short life was nearly over, but a gust of wind helped it flare hot one more time, and the needles, thin and lifeless, began to darken, almost imperceptibly at first, before they blackened and curled just a little. One tiny thread of smoke rose from where the cigarette kissed them.

CHAPTER 3

"WHOA! IT'S SPOILED MOVIE-STAR-WANNABE SWANN," SAID McKenzie. She wore denim shorts and a bikini top. "With Hunter the Wolf Slayer, his friend Kelton Lost-in-the-Woods Fielding, his girlfriend Annette, and his cousin Yummy."

"That seriously the best you can do?" Yumi said.

Annette watched the other group, openmouthed. Half of the reason she'd suggested this fishing trip was to get away from the war. The woods around McCall were nearly infinite, with hundreds of rivers, lakes, and ponds. How on earth had McKenzie Crenner's crowd chosen to come here? And what did it mean that Hunter hadn't objected to McKenzie calling her Hunter's girlfriend? *Doesn't matter, Annette! Get it together.*

Swann dropped her usual poise and confidence, slumping like a limp fish. "Come on," she said quietly, mostly to herself. "Now you guys have to copy us on our fishing trips?"

"What's that, Swanny?" McKenzie said. "Looks like you all have copied us."

"Are we fishing or what?" Mason Bridger shook his fishing pole and rattled his tackle box. He smiled. "Hey, Yumi."

Annette shot a wide-eyed look at her best friend. Yumi didn't meet her gaze. "Hi, Mason."

Morgan motioned toward the pond. "Nobody's saying you can't fish here too. It's not like there won't be enough room."

"Do you even fish, McKenzie?" Swann asked. "Or are you just trying to show off for Mason?"

"Oh, excuse me, Swanny," McKenzie fired back. "Is that what you all did in Hollywood? Go fishing? I've lived here all my life, and now you're going to show up and, like, act like the judge of who's legit in fishing? Seriously? Do you even hear yourself? Are you just so used to everybody doing what you say because your mommy and daddy have money? Well, sorry, Swanny." She tilted her head to the side and pouted in mock-sympathy. "We're not going to be your butler or maid or whatever other servants you're used to."

If McKenzie's words had hit home, Swann did a great job not showing it. Maybe she'd inherited some of her parents' acting skills. She kept a sincere-looking smile on her face the whole time. "Big speech, McKenzie," Swann said calmly. "Did you practice that before you came out here? You probably want to sit down and take a rest. That's a lot of words to string together for someone like you."

Annette winced at that one. Mason Bridger simply perched on a boulder beside the water, slipped a worm on his hook, and cast.

"This is stupid," Yumi said quietly. "Let's just fish already."

"Good idea," Annette said, leading the way down a worn dirt footpath that led around the opposite side of the pond from Mason. They marched through some tall grass, past the skeleton of a dead pine, and through a crack between a couple of large rocks, until they reached a pebbly beach with a handy old log for a seat.

"This would have been a perfect spot if the others weren't already here," Hunter said.

"I'm sorry, you guys. I had no idea," Annette said. "Today of all days they choose to come way out here?"

"They must have overheard us talking about this at the dance. So they grab the best fisher in the school and head out here," Swann said. "McKenzie just takes every chance she can to ruin everything and make things miserable."

Yumi opened her thermos and poured coffee into the screw-on cup top. "Well, she doesn't have to ruin this. Let's catch some fish."

At that moment, Morgan let out a little cheer while Mason Bridger tugged his line, let some out, and then reeled some in. He wasn't some newbie, fishing for the first time, who panicked at the first bite and cranked the reel for all he was worth until the line broke. He worked his fish well. McKenzie and Morgan acted almost like cheerleaders, but Mason was cool about it, eventually hoisting a little trout out of the lake. It was hard to tell from across the pond, but it looked about a foot long. Annette guessed it weighed about half a pound. Anyone who fished a lot became good at knowing a fish's weight judging by its length.

"They're cheering like they were the ones who caught it," Swann grumbled.

"Nice catch, Mason," Yumi called.

Swann and Kelton looked at her like she was a traitor, but Yumi shrugged. "What? We're going to pretend he didn't catch anything just because we're mad at McKenzie and Morgan?"

Swann sighed. "You're right. I shouldn't let her get to me. At my old school—"

"Oh, I'd rather die than hear about your old school," Yumi said with a laugh.

Swann laughed. "Yeah, OK. OK." Kelton squeezed her shoulder.

"Annette, what are we fishing for today?" Hunter asked.

Annette flashed Hunter a grin. Did he have any idea how grateful she was to him, not only for getting the group's focus shifted from their rivals across the pond, but also for treating her like an authority, for trusting that she actually knew about this sport she loved? Hunter loved going out in the woods to take game animals and was semi-famous, at least around school, for having shot a wolf. Kelton was all about snowmobiles. Fishing was Annette's big hobby. Well, fishing and writing. But it was hard to get together with friends to share writing.

"At this elevation, in a pond like this, we're fishing for trout," Annette said.

"I thought you were more into bass." Yumi sipped her coffee. "Didn't you and your dad participate in a bass-fishing tournament?"

"A couple of tournaments, actually," Annette agreed, smiling at the memory. But we'll have more luck with trout here. They're a little easier to catch. Bass are trickier. You have to work a little more to convince them to take the bait." Annette unzipped her backpack. "Trout will eat anything, and they especially go for shiny things, which is why I brought—"

More laughter echoed across Painted Pond. McKenzie pointed in their direction before saying something to Morgan and then laughing as she waddled around with her arms held out wide.

"What's that supposed to be about?" Swann said sharply.

"Just ignore them," Kelton said. When Swann spun to glare at him, he held his hands up. "Or not. You should definitely get really mad about it." McKenzie wound up like a baseball pitcher and hurled a golf ball-sized rock over the pond so that it splashed down right where Annette's group would be casting their lines.

"Come on," Mason said. "Quit messing around."

"Knock it off, losers." Swann yelled at them.

"Sorry," McKenzie yelled back. "It was an accident. So is this." She threw another rock.

"This is never going to work." Annette sighed. "They'll scare all the fish away. We'll never catch anything."

"Should we go back?" Kelton asked.

"You know," Swann said, "I never really cared about fishing that much. My dad and I fish from our new boat. It's fun, but I mostly like it for the chance to spend time with Dad. Mom comes sometimes too, but she mostly just relaxes or reads. Today

I thought it would at least be fun to hang out with you guys, but now?"

Yumi spoke in a near-growl. "Now you want to catch the biggest fish in Idaho, clean it, and make those rotten rejects eat the guts."

"Yeah. You get me," Swann said. "Mom's meditation guide wouldn't approve, but that's it exactly."

Hunter rested his fishing rod on his shoulder. "So what do we do?"

Annette pressed her lips together. Yumi and Hunter were right, and that was a pity. She loved this place for her memories of fishing with her dad and all the colorful pictures and words painted on the rock face. Modern-day cave art like she'd read about in her social studies textbook. Despite the vandalism, the pond itself remained pure. Clear, cold, and deep, ringed by rocks, a few trees, and small shrubs, a single stream running over rocks in and out of the pond. Painted Pond was supposed to be her group's little secret. The morning sun danced in a dazzling kaleidoscope of light as the surface was stirred up by a light but building breeze.

"There's another place we could go," Annette offered. "A place Dad and I used to fish that they won't know about. If you're up for more of a hike."

"I'm in," Yumi said. "We'll catch the biggest fish, and then take photos so those jerks across the water will know we outfished them."

"We can do even better than that." Swann gathered her gear

and moved closer to the pond. "Hey!" she shouted to the others. "We're going somewhere else to fish, since you're too afraid we'll catch all the big ones. But let's make it interesting. If we catch more and bigger fish, then we have permanent dibs on places in the future."

"Swann, what are you talking about?" Yumi hissed. "That's Mason Bridger over there. He's a fishing pro!"

Swann continued. "If we catch more and bigger fish today, you all promise to leave the area if we're ever in a situation like this again. And vice versa, but you'll never outfish us."

"Swann," Hunter whispered. "He won the Idaho title for biggest five-bass limit. Fished in the Big Bass Zone Junior Championship in Branson, Missouri."

"He goes fishing almost every day," Yumi said.

"Losers have to leave?" McKenzie called back.

"Well, you will always be the loser, so let's say, the team who catches fewer or smaller fish has to leave," said Swann.

"Swann?" Annette said. "This might not be a good idea. They're not kidding about Mason. He wins big money fishing. He even has corporate sponsors who give him free fishing poles, lures, and other gear."

"OK, you're on!" McKenzie waved at them from across the pond. "So go ahead and leave! You better get used to it."

Everyone gathered their belongings. Yumi tossed out the rest of the coffee in her cup. They all looked at Swann in varying degrees of shock. Kelton smiled like everything was normal, but Annette could tell his smile was forced.

"Oh, we're going to be clobbered," Hunter said.

"What?" Swann said. "Come on! Where's your spirit of adventure? We're like . . . the adventure men . . . or women. We can do anything. OK, so they have Mason Bridger. But he's like their only serious fisher. We have Annette as our guide. The rest of you are pretty good at all this nature stuff, and I'm ready to follow your lead. So . . . I guess . . . lead."

"The new place I'm thinking of is north of here on the Payette River," said Annette. "But it's like an hour hike away."

"No big deal," Hunter promised.

"You sure?" Yumi asked him. "With your leg—"

"Completely healed," Hunter snapped.

Yumi glanced from Hunter to Annette and back. "Oh. Right. I get it."

"You sure about this, everyone?" Annette asked. "If it's an hour up, it's an hour back down, plus the hike from Painted Pond back to the Gator and the drive."

Swann checked her phone. "It's way early. Let's go for it."

Annette worried that if they were out too late, her parents would return from work and discover she'd gone and taken the Gator.

Friendship favors the fun . . . and the foolish. Annette would have to write that down in her notebook once they were under way. "OK, then," she said. "Let's go win Swann's crazy bet. Let's go catch some fish."

CHAPTER 4

"BYE-BYE!" MCKENZIE CALLED AS HER RIVALS LEFT.

Annette led her group away from Painted Pond as quickly as she could, both to get away from the others and to make sure they had more fishing time, but the first part of the journey required a bit of a climb. There was something of a trail, more like a series of tight switchbacks landing on boulder after rock after stone ledge up the steep hill by the pond. Gradually Painted Pond shrank beneath them until finally they reached the top of the hill and picked up their pace along another barely visible trail.

They weren't quite running, because there were too many rocks along the way and they were all carrying fishing poles that sometimes snagged in the underbrush.

"Away from the pond, everything is brown," Swann said. "Like, everything."

"Not true," Kelton said playfully. "These dead shrubs are more of a reddish color."

"Shade of brown," said Swann.

Yumi pointed with her pole at a rock ridge rising as if the hill had an exposed spine. "The rocks are more gray."

"That's a shade of brown." Swann laughed a little.

"My mom takes some art classes to help her make better wine signs and other crap to sell at Wine O'Clock," Yumi said. "Her teacher is all about color theory. I don't understand half of what Mom says about it, but I'm pretty sure she'd disagree about gray being a shade of brown."

Swann laughed more. "Yumi, if I tell you something, will you promise not to get mad at me?"

"I will not promise that," Yumi said. "You have to take your chances with me."

"You do have to take your chances with her, though," Hunter called from the back of their single-file line.

"Shut it, Higgins!" Yumi said.

"Just that . . . those wine signs?" said Swann. "That say stuff like OH! LOOK AT THE TIME! IT'S WINE O'CLOCK AGAIN! or LIFE IS WHAT HAPPENS BETWEEN COFFEE AND WINE or—"

Yumi cut in. "Or I COOK WITH WINE. SOMETIMES I EVEN ADD IT TO THE FOOD. Yeah, what about them?"

"When we first moved to McCall, my Mom hired a decorator and asked her to add rustic highlights."

Annette frowned, intrigued. She couldn't imagine hiring an outsider to decorate her home. Her house had some family photos and, years ago, crappy crayon drawings her little brother had made. "What are rustic—"

"Yeah, I don't know what that means either," Swann

admitted. "But this woman showed up with a crate full of those wine signs, and I had to try to distract my mom and get her to change the subject because she was laughing and hurting the designer's feelings.

"My mother makes a ton of money on those signs," Yumi said evenly. Annette pressed her lips together. *Come on, Yumi. It's not a big deal. Let's keep this friendly.* Yumi continued, "She makes the signs herself. Works hard on them."

There was a long silence, filled only by the sound of their footsteps crunching in the dry grass. One of them snapped a twig.

"Well," Swann said, "I didn't think . . . you know, Mom *loves* your mom's store. Buys wine by the case there."

Yumi stopped and turned to face Swann, a serious expression burning on her face. "Those signs"—Yumi smiled—"are the dumbest things I've ever seen!" She burst out laughing. "And you should have seen the look on your face, Swann!" She laughed more, and soon everybody else joined in. "Mom hates them too, but she makes crazy money on them. Sometimes I help make the signs. Mom lets me keep some of the cash. Once I just stenciled WINE in black letters on a crappy scrapwood plank. She sold it to some chump from . . . um . . . a certain southwestern coastal state . . . for forty dollars!"

They followed a gentle path down the back slope of the hill and wound through a valley shaded by pines, where they walked on a soft carpet of dry orange pine needles. A quiet place, save for the occasional crunch when one of them stepped on a pine cone. But the still peace felt like a living force, almost a tangible power that calmed them and invited them to focus on who they were, on who they were with, and above all on the bright relief and fresh untouched purity of the natural world around them.

"The shade is nice." Swann spoke in nearly a whisper. Annette understood her reluctance to disturb the wilderness. Swann continued, "Sun's heating right up."

Annette smiled at her, and then slowed to take a look at everyone else. "I see Kelton, Hunter, and Yumi have CamelBaks for drinking water. I wish I had brought something to drink besides soda. We're going to need water."

Hunter nodded. "The Payette River's pretty clean. I have a water filter pump in my backpack just to make sure it's safe."

"Aren't *you* the always prepared Boy Scout," Yumi said.

"Not a Boy Scout," Hunter said. "It's just a new pump I got for camping, and I thought this would be a good chance to try it out. Glad I brought it now."

Kelton sucked some water from the tube that ran over his shoulder from his pack. "Mom said she found a good deal on my CamelBak. Since we, you know, almost died in the wilderness, she's been all about getting me better outdoor gear. I even have a proper first-aid kit. Real bandages and everything."

"Which, I didn't think we'd need all that stuff," Annette said. "We were only taking one simple trail to Painted Pond."

"You thirsty?" Kelton wiped the drinking knob of his CamelBak tube on his sleeve and held it out to Swann.

"You drink from that, and it will be just like kissing him,"

Yumi said. Swann rolled her eyes, and stepped closer to Kelton, taking the drinking tube in hand. Yumi chuckled. "His mouth has been all over that. You're seriously going to do it?"

Swann glanced at Yumi, then fixed Kelton with an intense gaze for a moment before smiling. In the next instant, she pulled Kelton close and, closing her eyes, kissed him on the lips.

Kelton's eyes went wide for a moment, and then he made a soft little moan before closing them and—Annette didn't know how to describe it—getting into the spirit of the kiss. "Whoa," was all Kelton said when their lips parted. Swann stayed close to him and giggled. Then she winked at him before holding up his drinking tube with a smile.

She took a good long pull of water. "Wonderful."

"Wow." Yumi laughed. "I was just making a bad joke about the drinking being just like kissing. I can't believe you did that."

"Me neither," Kelton said. He added quickly, "I'm not complaining, though. Yumi, you go right on telling bad jokes."

They resumed walking. If Swann and Kelton hadn't kissed right there in front of her, Annette probably wouldn't have believed it had happened. Watching them, she felt . . . not jealous, exactly. Jealous was when someone had something you wanted and you wanted that person to suffer or to lose whatever it was that she had. Annette was happy for Swann and Kelton. Kelton Fielding! That must have been some snowmobile trip, for a guy who had so often been the outsider to end up with a girl Annette knew for a fact was the subject of many of the guys' crushes.

Annette simply wondered what it would be like to have a boyfriend. She'd never kissed a boy, and she wondered how that felt. But it was more than that. With that kiss, Swann had declared to them all, and maybe to Kelton too, judging by his surprised expression, that the two of them were together. They belonged together and could share things like that water tube. And kisses. They were each other's favorite person. Annette would love to be someone's favorite.

She glanced at Hunter, who kept pace with her, just a little bit behind her on her right. He smiled. Why was he so cute when he smiled? His sandy brown hair was always just a bit messed up, like he was always more interested in the next big outdoor adventure than in getting a haircut. He was kind of short, even for the end of summer before seventh grade. And he was a little stocky, not too much. Just solid. Some of the boys had started lifting weights. Would he be one of them? How would Hunter look with his muscles all puffed up? Her cheeks were red. She hoped everyone would think that was merely due to the hike and the heat of the day.

"How you doing, Slayer?" she asked. Where had that come from? She almost never called him Slayer. She loved the way his name sounded. "Hunter."

"Good." He moved up to walk along beside her. The trail was narrow, so they had to walk close. "We still on course?"

"Sure," Annette said, certain of that much, at least. "My father and I used to take this route a lot. Still a ways to go, but we're not lost, if that's what you mean."

"Oh no," Hunter said quickly, "that's not what I was getting at. I just meant, like, is everything good and are we getting closer. You know, like how adults will see you doing homework and say something like, *You getting through it?* I should have just asked you what's up."

Why hadn't she understood him? Why did everything with Hunter Higgins have to be so complicated? *Just act normal!* "Sure," she said. "It stinks we had to leave Painted Pond, but it's great to be out here."

"You, um . . ." Hunter began.

Annette waited for a long moment for him to continue. "I . . . what?"

A few paces behind them, Yumi and Swann were talking about some video game. Maybe the two of them being busy with that gave Hunter the courage to continue.

"You remember the welcome-back-to-middle-school dance?"

Annette laughed a little, and took her eyes off the trail to look at Hunter. He did not meet her gaze. His cheeks were red, though from the hike and growing heat or from embarrassment, she couldn't tell. "The dance last night? Yes, I remember."

"Yeah." He spoke slowly and deliberately. "Duh. Of course you remember. I just meant that at that dance . . . well, your dress was real good." Then he hurried to finish. "It was a real nice dress."

She bit her lip to hold in her laughter. Hunter Higgins was trying to compliment her. Nobody ever complimented her, not even teachers, who were no longer surprised by, but merely expected, good schoolwork from her. She certainly wasn't ever praised by boys. And he was so embarrassed trying to say all this. She needed to help him relax.

"Thanks. It was my sister's dress."

"Well, it looked—*you* looked—really pretty."

Her heart beat heavier. She swallowed. He was so sweet. "Thank you," she said quietly.

"Yumi said I should tell you that," Hunter said. When Annette looked at him, he shook his head and quickly added, "But I . . . I . . . you know, thought it. Myself. I thought it, told Yumi, she said—"

Now Annette did laugh. "I get it. Thank you."

The group climbed another mildly challenging rise and took a moment to rest on top of the ridge. They were above the trees, above the whole world it seemed, except for the larger mountains in the hazy distance.

"Too bad the sky out there has to be so brown," Yumi said.

"Smoke from fires in Montana," Kelton said.

"I thought the smoke was from fires in Oregon," Hunter said.

"What difference does it make?" Yumi said. "It looks gross, and sad. And it's like this every summer."

Swann held her hand out toward the expansive view. "Yeah, but even if it's a little hazy, look at that. I was talking to Cynthia this last school year, back during the worst part of the war. And I . . . I'll just be honest with you all, that was a really crappy time. People were posting some terrible things, about me and about some of you, online and it bothered me. Anyway, Cynthia said"—Swann spoke slowly, as if concentrating to recite from memory—"that even if it's not fair, and especially if it's difficult, to get by in life, to, um, not merely survive but to *live*, we have to force ourselves to recognize the good things."

"I like that," Kelton said.

"Of course you do," Yumi said. "Swann said it."

"Well, that's part of it, yeah," Kelton agreed. "But, I mean, even though we're doing better, money's still tight for me and my mom. Sometimes it gets me down, but I got my dog Scruffy now." He took a deep satisfied breath. Then he smiled and motioned toward everybody. "And then there's, you know, all of this. Focusing on the good stuff may not make problems go away, but—"

"But if we focus on the bad stuff, it's too easy to lose sight of the good," Swann said.

"And that gets you real down, real quick," Kelton said.

"Oh, you two are completing each other's sentences now?" Yumi cut in. "That's disgustingly cute."

They laughed and continued on their way back down the other side of the ridge into a valley through which ran a swift-running creek. "This spills into the Payette River," Annette said. The creek rushed over and around rocks, low in its course. Annette pointed at a white line at least three feet higher than the current water level. "In spring and early summer, the water's a lot higher here."

"The last of the melted mountain snowpack coming down," Hunter said.

Some small trout moved swiftly through the clear creek. "Bigger trout in the river. Plus smallmouth bass and even some salmon," Annette said. "It's not far. Right where this creek reaches the river."

The hike was simple following the creek. They all moved faster, eager to get their hooks in the water. At last they approached the river and reached the secret spot.

"We're here," Annette said. The creek spilled into the river. Right downstream from that point a bridge crossed the water. She always thought it looked incredibly elaborate for a country footbridge. On either bank of the river, silver-painted girders rose from concrete abutments. Steel cables sagged over the span between the girders, supporting a walking surface two wood planks wide.

"It's like the Golden Gate Bridge in San Francisco," Swann said. "Only super-small, and silver instead of orange."

Yumi stepped out onto the planks a few paces before turning back to face the group. "I don't get it. Bridge to nowhere? Why is this here?"

The nearby gravel parking lot was mostly overgrown, so Annette wasn't surprised Yumi had missed it. Annette pointed to a trail that wound up over the hill on the far bank. "There's a cabin over there. This lot is as close as anyone can park. They walk from here." Annette addressed the unspoken question. "Yes, we could have hiked all the way back to the Gator and driven clear around, but it would have taken a lot longer than hiking overland, and we'd run the risk of getting caught driving the Gator."

"Sweet." Kelton looked around. With the river, creek, parking lot, and trail, the trees were back a little. Still, being so close to plenty of water, the pines on the perimeter were huge and tall, throwing some shade.

"Water's usually a little deeper here where the creek joins the river by the bridge," Annette explained. "The shade helps with the fishing too."

"And best of all," Swann said, "no McKenzie and company to ruin it."

Hunter looked down the long driveway to where it bent in the undergrowth. "No car, so the cabin owners must not be home."

"No adults," Yumi said. "It's just us out here."

Annette took a seat on the warm smooth wood planks in the middle of the suspension bridge, and pulled her tackle box from her backpack. "Like I was trying to say back at Painted Pond before we were interrupted, trout go for shiny things. And we're going for a reaction bite, meaning we're going to move the lure to look like a little tasty creature, as opposed to just deadsticking it, casting the line and leaving it more still until there's a bite."

Swann sat down beside her. "How did you learn all this?"

"Practice." Annette began tying a spinner on her own line, noticing Swann watching her work the improved fisherman's knot. "My dad and I used to go fishing all the time. I've caught hundreds of fish." When she'd tied on her own spinner with its hairy little fake bug around the hook and the shiny blade dangling from the end of the adjacent wire arm, she offered everyone else the choice between fishing with a simple worm or using a spinner like her. Everybody except Yumi chose the spinner, following her example. She worked quickly to set up Hunter and Kelton.

"So you really know all about fishing," Swann said after Annette tied on a couple of spinners.

"No," Annette said. "Others, like Mason back there? They know everything about fishing. I just love it, the sport of it. The challenge. Figuring out what sort of fish are likely in the water, the best way to catch them. It's as much of an art as writing."

"You make it almost sound like a poem," Swann said.

Yumi sat down beside Annette opposite from Swann, grabbing a worm from Annette's coffee can, sticking it on her hook, and casting. "Roses are red. Violets are blue. I want to start fishing. And so should you."

She'd said it kind of grumpy, but they all laughed a little, and then cast into the river to finally begin fishing.

RIGHT OFF THE SMALL SANDY SHOULDER OF EASTSIDE DRIVE, north of Lake Payette, one last tiny orange ember, a speck at the end of the discarded cigarette, flared a little brighter in the breeze. The blackened pine needle upon which the cigarette rested curled up, orange needle turned to black and then orange again in a flame no larger than a fingernail.

The flame crawled in both directions down the needle, and onto the next needles. A little hotter now, the white paper of the cigarette butt browned, blackened, and burst into tiny flame. The wind gusted again, whispering through the pines overhead, and the burning cigarette rolled several feet, lighting other pine needles twice on the way before coming to rest next to a cluster of pine cones. There the flames on the cigarette nearly died, until they were boosted by the ignition of the pine needles beneath it.

Now the fire from where the cigarette had just landed grew hungry, past its timid slow struggle to ignite. It searched for more food, more fuel, and spread in an orange ring over a foot from where it had started. Burning more. Gaining speed.

The cigarette was gone, consumed by its own fire, which ignited a clump of eight large dry pine cones. The pine cones burned quickly, and hot. The leaves of a shrubbery hanging above them browned and blackened, curled and then burned, so that the yellow-orange flames seemed to dance from leaf to leaf, branch to branch. The fire spread from the pine cones up the slope under the burning leaves. The wind gusted, the ashes flared red in delight, the ring of fire surged up the hill a little faster, and light smoke rose into the already hazy air.

CHAPTER 5

JUST BECAUSE YUMI HAD ALWAYS LIVED IN MCCALL, A town people visited to experience the wilderness, didn't mean she loved every outdoor activity. She liked hunting, but not as much as others in her family. She loved archery and shooting rifles. Swimming and skiing were fun, in their separate seasons. And it was great to simply be out in the wild, hiking and exploring.

She hadn't been fishing for about three years. As she sat with her feet dangling off the suspension footbridge a few feet above the river, a lot of memories came back to her. She remembered that she didn't like fishing that much. Now she was reminded of why.

Most of fishing was simply staring at the water, despite what Annette said. Her dad would condemn her lack of adventure spirit for saying so, but video games were more fun. There was always something happening in one of her games. As she watched the water below, there was nothing to do but wait.

How did Annette get so into fishing? And Annette barely counted in fishing compared to Mason Bridger. Mason went fishing nearly every day, except for some of the coldest winter days. He literally was a pro, getting paid to fish. Yumi, on the other hand, had mostly agreed to go fishing just to be with the group.

"This is great," Annette said quietly, slowly reeling in her line a little.

What was so great about this? If Swann hadn't made that stupid bet with McKenzie they could have ditched the fishing plan and just hiked in the woods, gone out to see someplace they'd never seen before.

"Fishing is more than a simple sport," Annette continued lazily. "It's all about going to a place away from other people, to be alone."

Yumi couldn't resist cutting into her speech. "There are five of us here."

"Alone with other people," Hunter said. "You know what she means."

Hunter and Annette were getting along better and better all the time. Ever since Annette came hunting with them last fall, she and Hunter had a certain weirdness between them. Annette was one of the most interesting and open people Yumi had ever met—about everything except who she liked. She'd had a crush once and kept it secret, but now it was pretty clear she liked Hunter. And since there was basically nobody Yumi knew as well as Hunter, she was positive he liked her. Neither of them had the courage to admit that to the other yet, and Yumi was tired of playing go-between, trying to make that happen. At least the two of them were finally acting more at ease with each other than they had since they all set out this morning.

"Fishing is great to relax, you know?" Annette said. "To be with nature, and catch some fish."

"But why do we have to catch fish to be with nature?" Yumi asked. "I'm not complaining, but trying to understand. We could have just hiked out here to go swimming or something."

"Maybe it's like when my dad is working out some story issue for a movie he's working on," said Swann. "Sometimes he's stuck, trying to figure out the next thing, so he paces his office, carrying this pure smooth piece of lapis lazuli. I asked him once, and he said that the movement plus keeping his hands busy with the stone free up his mind to do his best thinking."

Hunter leaned back so he could see past Annette and look at Yumi. "Kind of like when you're stumped on some question on your homework, but then you'll come up with the answer when you're playing a video game."

"I take video game breaks just because I like video games," Yumi said.

Annette's reel clicked slowly and rhythmically as she cranked the handle. "One of my favorite authors, Tammy Pren, who writes the Mystic Realms books—"

"I love those books," Swann said.

"I've always wanted to play the Mystic Realms tabletop game," Kelton said. "You know, with the little figures." Swann gently elbowed him quiet.

Annette smiled, looking at the water. "I watched an

interview of Tammy Pren online. She says she can always think better when she goes for walks in the woods with her favorite old polished wooden walking stick, sipping coffee." Annette sat up straight when her line suddenly jerked taut, but it was only a nibble. The fish must have avoided taking the lure. "There's something about engaging in an easy physical task that opens our minds to thinking better."

Yumi watched the water. Annette was pretty great, but sometimes, like when she'd thrown gas on the fire of the war by jumping in the middle with her let's-all-get-along article, she could be a bit too much. Be with nature? Open our minds? Where did she come up with this stuff?

A tiny quick tightness on Yumi's line. The pole barely jerked. "Got a little nibble there," she said. Then the line went tight, the pole was pulled. "Think I got one!"

"All right, Yumi!" Kelton said. "Reel that in!"

The fish was fighting for it, pulling a lot harder than the tiny one she remembered catching with her dad years ago. "He's not giving up." Yumi laughed. Of course, she who was the least interested would be the first to catch anything. The surface of the river splashed. A flash of fin.

"Trout really flop around a lot," Annette said.

"Think you have kind of a big one," Hunter said.

"Oh no, little fishy buddy." She giggled. This was more exciting than she thought it would be, kind of a rush to be in a prolonged fight against this living thing. Unlike hunting a deer from a distance with a rifle, her prey was now connected to her on the other end of that line. They shared a physical struggle. "You can't get away. Come on. I got you."

After more hand cranks of the reel and a final jerk of the pole, the fish burst up out of the water. It folded itself almost in half, first one way, then the other.

Hunter rushed to his feet, pulling himself up with the metal rail and jerking back his hand. "Ouch. Watch that steel. Plenty hot in the sun."

"You OK?" Annette asked.

Yumi rolled her eyes. Of course Higgins was fine. He'd acted like a baby when touching a bit of hot metal. It wasn't like his hand had been shoved in a fire.

Hunter grabbed Yumi's fishing line, yanking up to take pressure off the rod. "You got a big one here, Cousin."

OK. Maybe fishing was a little fun. Yumi smiled. "I thought the pole was going to break. How far can these things bend?"

"No, you were good," Annette said. "They can bend far. I know they look like they're going to snap, but they're designed to bend. Looks like you got a sweet trout there."

"Wow, that's awesome!" Swann reached over and squeezed Yumi's shoulder.

In middle school, and especially during the war, Yumi had learned the hard way to play it cool and not let people see how interested she was in something. Too often, any display of interest was merely an invitation for people to make fun of whatever it was she liked. Swann was different. Sometimes she seemed like a kid who was excited about everything, like someone excited for Christmas and reindeer and Santa Claus. Yeah, it was a little annoying, but there was also something encouraging and refreshing about her attitude.

Annette pulled her dad's old spring-loaded fish scale from her backpack and hung Yumi's catch beneath it. "Just like I thought. Almost a pound and a half. Not bad."

"What do we do now?" Swann said. "Are we going to eat him?"

"I've never had sushi. I'm not sure how they make it," Kelton said. "But I bet it's not made of trout."

"Well, we can cook it, right?" Swann asked. "We just make a fire and—"

"Whoa!" Annette said.

"Yeah," Kelton said. "No, that's not going to work."

"Heck, no," Hunter said.

Yumi stared at her in disbelief. "Don't they have wildfires all the time in California?"

"Yeah," Swann said, a little defensively. "So?"

"Swann." Annette sounded more understanding. "We're deep into the burn ban. The fine for lighting even a little cook fire would be huge."

"Nobody's out here," Swann said. "Who would catch us?"

Kelton looked reluctant to disagree with her. "But as dry as everything is, if that fire got out of control, the whole county would flame up. The astronauts could literally see the smoke from space." He must have noticed Swann's look of disbelief. "I'm serious. I saw it on a video online."

"What's the big deal? We light the fire right next to the river, inches from the water, sitting on a rock." Swann tried again. "We'd be right there to splash water on it if there were any problems."

She was really serious. Yumi reminded herself that it wasn't Swann's fault that she grew up rich in a big city. "It seems like that would make sense. But if one tiny hot piece of ash floats away out of the fire and comes down on some of those dry pine needles, it can start a major fire faster than you think."

Annette held up the scale and Yumi's trout. "Swann? Photo?"

"Oh yeah." Swann pulled out her phone and snapped a quick picture of the fish. "No service out this far to send it to that brat. We'll have to bomb her with the full batch when we're back in a coverage area." She put her phone away. "Are you serious about the fire stuff, though?"

"It is very serious," Hunter said. "Especially in the dry summer forests around McCall."

"That John Deere Gator?" Annette took the fish off the hook and reached it down over the edge of the bridge as low as she could before dropping it. With a splash it was gone, speeding off beneath the surface of the cool water. "By law, to run that machine out here, the exhaust has to have a special Forest Service–approved spark arrester."

"Same on my family's four-wheelers," Hunter said. "Super-tiny sparks can shoot out of a normal exhaust system. If it sparks over dry grass or pine needles, it can start a fire. A rider might be miles away before he realizes he started the fire, and by that time it could be way out of control."

"Even just the normal heat from under a car that parks in tall dry grass can start a fire," Kelton added.

"How, though?" Swann asked. "The spark thing I guess I understand, but just a normal car or truck?"

"I saw a whole vid—"

"Video about it online," Swann said. "Yeah, I know." She held up her hands in surrender. "OK. OK. No fires. I'll write that down. And I thought being out in these mountains in the winter could be dangerous. All of that snow seems like baby stuff compared to your fire fears."

"Don't say that." Hunter chuckled, rubbing the leg he'd broken when taking shelter from the blizzard in an abandoned mine. "Don't you ever say that."

They fished some more.

Hunter coughed to cover his laugh and Yumi struggled to contain herself when Kelton cast his line from his tiny kiddie fishing pole. The rod was a gold color, its handle and reel a bright red. A faded picture of Iron Man brightened one side.

His spinner plopped down in the river below and he frowned as he glanced at Yumi and Hunter. "What? You laughing at my fishing pole?"

Everybody but Swann laughed. "Kind of," Annette admitted.

Swann frowned. "Not everybody can buy an expensive—"

"It's OK, Swann." Kelton smiled at her and held up a hand. To the others he added, "What? Iron Man isn't cool anymore? After everything he did for us, sacrificing his life to save us from

Thanos? You all should be ashamed of yourselves. For real." He had cranked his line all the way in. He cast again. "I. Am. Iron Man. And I'm going to catch the biggest fish."

Almost as if the fish had heard him, Kelton's line jerked taut with a bite. He reeled it in. Yumi frowned. She didn't know as much about fishing as Annette, but even she could tell this was too easy. Kelton kept reeling in, and a moment later a tiny four-inch-long fish dangled at the end of his line. Everyone, even Kelton, laughed.

"Way to go, Iron Man," Yumi said. She was happy to see Kelton laughing with them. It wasn't so long ago that the guy took every criticism, even friendly jokey ones, so personally. Something had happened to Kelton, Swann, and Higgins last winter on Storm Mountain. Something important.

"Anybody thirsty?" Swann asked. "Doesn't matter. There's five of us, and I have five cans of Coke, and they aren't getting any colder."

Annette perked up. "Right. I have five cans of root beer. And a bag of chips!"

Kelton pulled his plastic pouch of beef jerky from his pack. "I don't know if I should let you all have any of this after you insulted my fishing pole, but . . . I guess."

Swann grabbed her sodas from her backpack and then produced the candy bars. "Snickers?"

"Oh, awesome, Swann," Annette said. "Thanks!"

Yumi watched the other two girls. When had they become so friendly? The group divided up the treats. Yumi was grateful for the chips and candy bar, but she would have brought something if she had known this was going to be a picnic.

Not much happened with the fish for a while after that. It was the kind of boring fishing Yumi remembered.

"That's the way it goes sometimes," Annette said. "You can fish a spot one day and big fish will be biting the whole time. Next day. Same spot. Same bait. But nothing."

"Nothing is right." Yumi sighed.

"So, anyway," Swann said, after a bit of silence. Why did some people think every quiet moment needed to be filled with talk? Swann continued, "School starting next week."

"Oh, why you gotta say that?" Hunter whined.

"Because," Swann said, "I want to know if you guys are going out for football. It's the first year you can play on the school team, right?"

"That's true," Kelton said. "Jack Dunning and Tannin Gravin are super-excited about it. A lot of guys were talking about it at the end of the last school year."

"Yeah," said Hunter. "It seemed like that's all anyone talked about. Football, football, football."

"Are you really not going out for football?" Yumi asked. This wasn't the first time the two of them had talked about this. Hunter had made it clear he wasn't very interested in it. But McCall was a real small town. It wasn't like one of those giant big-city schools she'd seen in movies, the ones where people had to try out in a competition to make the team. In McCall, and, she was pretty sure, all the schools McCall played against, if someone was interested in a sport, he just joined the team. Especially in football, the coach would use anyone he could get, as a backup at the very least. For the boys even more than for the girls, the decision to *not* go out for a sport was noticed. Grandpa and Uncle David kind of expected Hunter to be on the football team in the fall.

"I don't know," Hunter said. "I still haven't decided."

"Me neither," Kelton said. He sounded relieved and shot a smile at Hunter. Maybe he was happy he was no longer alone about doubting football. "My mom says I can, but I can tell she's worried. She's been reading these articles about the dangers of concussions from football."

"Oh yeah," said Swann. "My mom was saying she can't believe football is still allowed. Most of the sons of her friends would never be allowed."

Hunter frowned. "It's not *that* dangerous. Some people act like you'll explode if you play football. It's not that bad. Zillions of people play it and are just fine."

Yumi smiled. There was Higgins, who hated football more than he would say, defending it because outsiders had criticized it. She understood completely.

"Oh, don't get me wrong," Swann said. "I think it's cool. I don't understand the game that much, but it looks fierce. And it's so different from my old—"

Yumi watched her. Swann had stopped herself from talking about her old school. She was learning.

Swann continued, "I'm thinking about trying volleyball."

Yumi smiled. "Me too." It would be great to have a friend on the team. If Swann was a friend. She could tell by the way Annette remained focused on her fishing that she had no interest in volleyball. "That's kind of McKenzie's main thing. Volleyball and basketball. But who cares, right? We'll have fun. We'll do fine."

Swann high-fived her.

"I might give football a try," Kelton said. "I don't know much about it, but there's bound to be some YouTube videos about how to play the game. It could be fun."

Swann leaned way over, nearly lying down in Kelton's lap. "You and your videos." She smiled up at him. "You master the whole world with those things." They looked at each other for a long moment.

Yumi coughed loudly, fearing they were going to kiss. "We're *fishing* here."

Hunter reeled his line all the way in. "Yeah, but so far, not much luck. Maybe I need to try something different? Would just a worm work better?"

"I doubt it," Annette said. "Just keep trolling. Trout are all about movement. But you could try it. Sometimes something like that works for seemingly no reason."

"Maybe I should switch to worms," Swann said. "This spinner isn't working."

Annette removed the spinner from Hunter's line, pulled a worm from her can, and reached over toward Hunter, their fingers brushing as she went to put the worm on the hook.

"Hunter, stay *still*." She put her hand on his, long enough to hook the worm, and then a little longer.

Annette finally let go of Hunter, and he just stared at his hands, smiling like an idiot. She pointed downstream to a big round gray boulder in the shade of a stand of pines. "You might try fishing off the top of that rock. I've had some luck there in the past. I'm not giving up here, though. I'll stay on the bridge for a while at least."

"Yeah, I'll stay too," Hunter said quickly. He met Kelton's gaze and gave a little nod.

Oh no. Yumi groaned. Did Hunter think he was being sneaky? Like nobody else saw that? Had the two boys talked and planned this whole fishing trip out as some kind of date? Kelton and Swann were clearly together. Yumi was ninety percent sure Hunter and Annette liked each other. Was the boys' idea to use this trip to make everything official for both couples? Which, good for them. She wanted both couples to be happy. It would be nice if Hunter and Annette would get over their shyness and just admit to liking each other already, but that was a different issue. The problem, if her cousin and best friend had arranged with Kelton to make this whole thing a date-type of situation, was that it would be a date for two couples. *Couples!* Leaving Yumi, as usual, the oddball. The third wheel. Or *fifth* wheel in this situation. Fifth wheels had to do with hauling large trailers, and once again, it would be she, Yumi, suffering the burden on this trip.

"Maybe I'll try fishing from the top of that rock," Kelton said.

"Want company?" Swann asked. The two of them gathered their gear and stood to leave.

Yumi sighed. "You know what? I'm going with them. Have some better luck maybe."

Was that disappointment on Kelton and Swann's faces? She couldn't be sure. On Kelton's maybe, but Swann, the daughter of an actor and actress, was a master at hiding or faking her true feelings.

Yumi followed Swann and Kelton off the bridge and along the bank of the river. They walked side by side, and closer than they had before. Yumi knew she couldn't win this. Her choice was to fish alone like a weirdo, or to be in the way of one of the two couples.

"Fishing was pretty fun with my dad," Swann said. "It's been part of his effort to spend more time with me, and it's been wonderful. But we fish from our boat, and we're both just kind of there. He drives the boat around the lake and lets me drive sometimes, which is great. But that's it, you know?"

"What do you mean, that's it?" Kelton said. "You're talking about an incredible brand-new deluxe twenty-foot fishing boat. That's not enough?"

Swann laughed as if everything Kelton said was funny.

"The boat's great. But in a way, it's kind of confining." Swann held her fishing pole up high, slowly spinning around once, as though making a grand gesture to the whole world. "But out here! We explore the world *and* fish at the same time. Look at this place. I could live out here. Seriously. I wish that cabin over the hill was mine so we could just live here for a week. Live here all summer."

"Makes sense," Yumi said. "It's different fishing from the bridge, or standing on the shore, or from up on the rock."

"Exactly." Swann smiled at her. "You get me."

Yumi doubted that very much, but what Swann had said about the fun of being out exploring the wilderness was understandable enough.

It was a trick for the three of them, with all their gear, to climb atop the boulder, and once they were at the top, there wasn't a lot of room. That was probably fine for Swann and Kelton, but now, in addition to crowding into their conversation, Yumi was physically crowding them as well.

Yumi whipped her pole hard to cast, her lure splashing into the water far on the other side of the stream.

"Wow!" Kelton said. "Nice one, Yumi. You look like one of the pros from the fishing videos."

Yumi laughed. "If I catch anything."

In the next instant, she felt the hard tug of a bite. "Whoa." She hadn't even sat down yet, so the tug of the fish on the line had pulled her off balance a little. Swann grabbed hold of her to steady her. "Thanks," Yumi said, reeling in the fish. This wasn't any tiny thing like Kelton had hooked earlier. She'd have to work this one a little. She let out some line to take pressure off her rod, then reeled the fish in a little. A little more.

"Awesome, Yumi," Kelton said. "You're our best hope of winning the bet."

Her pole bent, but Yumi took her time bringing the fish in. A beautiful trout splashed out of the water. She brought it up until she could grab hold and lift it up for Annette and Hunter to see.

"Way to go, Yumi!" Annette called to her from the bridge. "I told you that's a good spot. Want me to bring the scale? Or you can just measure it. I have an app that will compute the weight."

"I don't have a tape measure," Yumi admitted.

Swann rose to her feet, holding her phone up. "I'll use the measuring app. Hold the fish still."

The fish wasn't interested in staying still, but Yumi did her best.

"Twenty-two inches," Swann called out.

Annette tapped her phone. "Two-point-two-three pounds!"

"Awesome," Hunter said. "Make sure you get a picture to send to McKenzie."

"Here, I got it," Swann snapped another photo. "Good one, Yumi. You're the best."

But she was not the best after that. First Kelton, then Annette, then Swann caught fish, all just as large as or bigger than Yumi's.

They were supposed to be all working together fishing against McKenzie's group, but instead they had divided into couples. Hunter and Annette. Swann and Kelton. Yumi by herself, with barely enough room to remain on top of the stupid rock. After about an hour and a half, she'd had enough.

"You know," Yumi said to Swann and Kelton, "I'm going to try something different."

"Oh, are you sure?" Swann said. She didn't sound like she much cared what Yumi did.

Yumi didn't tell her what she really had in mind. She didn't want to cause a big thing.

"Yeah." Yumi started to climb down. "If you could just hand me my gear." But once she was down, she kept waiting. "Seriously, you guys, could one of you hand down my stuff?"

"Oh sorry, Yumi," Kelton said. Kelton lowered her pole and then lay on his belly atop the rock to reach down with her CamelBak pack and thermos. "I thought I had another bite, so I was kind of focused on that."

"Yeah, I know you're very focused," Yumi said. *Focused on Swann.* But the guy looked so happy. Smiling like an idiot. And people had been really crappy to Kelton. Even she and Hunter hadn't been very good friends with him through the last couple of years. It was good for him to be close to someone, to have friends and a girlfriend.

Why couldn't she ever have anyone? What was so bad about her? Yumi went back toward the bridge, and for just a moment thought about returning to fish with Hunter and Annette, but they were sitting kind of close, and finally talking. About what? Yumi had no idea. But she didn't want to interrupt. At least not very much.

"Hey, you two, I'm going to head back," Yumi said. Annette and Hunter hadn't heard her as she approached. When neither of them responded to her, she spoke again. "Annette, I'm heading back."

Annette sat up straight. "What? Back where?"

"Don't be crazy, Yumi," Hunter said. "You can't go by yourself."

"Relax, Higgins," she said. "It's not like your winter avalanche nightmare. The trail was pretty clear the whole way here. I can find Painted Pond. From there, no problem."

"Yeah, but it's so far," Annette said. "Are you not having fun?"

Oh no. If Annette started to make a big hurt deal out of this, she'd never get away, and the two of them would be talking about this for weeks. She had to handle this just right. "You kidding me? I've caught two sweet trout! Don't think this is the last time we're doing this. Our fishing team will return. I just need to help my mom with some stuff at the store. I didn't think we'd be out this long. Of course, none of us knew there would already be people at Painted Pond."

Hunter frowned and grabbed the handrail in a sunny spot to pull himself up, only to jerk his arm back in surprise. "Darn it! Hot!" He started to rise again. "Yumi, you really shouldn't go through the woods by yourself. You never know—"

"Higgins, I think that wolf has gone to your head," Yumi shot back. "You aren't the only one who can handle the wilderness. I'll be fine. Seriously."

"Are you sure?" Annette said.

"Ann." Yumi put her hands on her hips. "You fish. I'm going. Goodbye."

Without another word, she set off at a fast pace, not running, but seriously moving. In her head, she didn't want to deal with the two couples anymore. But a part of her, a bigger part than she would have ever admitted, even to herself, was more than a little disappointed that her friends didn't try harder to make her stay.

CHAPTER 6

ANNETTE WATCHED HER BEST FRIEND HURRY AWAY UNTIL she vanished through a stand of dense shrubs and pine trees. "Is she really going to be OK?"

"She was driving the snowmobile when you two came up Storm Mountain to save us, right?" Hunter asked. He pushed a strand of his hair out of his face.

"Yeah, she was driving." The heat had to be up into the nineties by now, or else very close. It was the opposite of that scary snowy day.

"See?" Hunter gently bumped her with his shoulder. "She knows what she's doing. Yumi's tough."

Annette laughed. Why had he bumped her? What did that mean? That was flirting, right? And that meant what Yumi'd said was true and he really did like her, right? Then what? She couldn't just tell him that she liked him. Dad had joked once about how when he was in school back in the 1900s, he had written a paper note to a girl that said something like, *I like you. Do you like me? Circle YES or NO.* It wasn't like that now. Her father barely even had internet when he was a little kid. This was the twenty-first century. And that meant . . . she had no idea. About anything.

Or was she overthinking everything again? Worrying too much? This was Hunter, after all. They'd talked so much when taking a break from hunting outside his family's lodge last fall. He was a good guy. *Just talk to him!* "Did I ever tell you how cool I think it is that you two cousins are so close?"

"Hmm," Hunter said. "Once or twice. I know she thinks you're awesome." He touched his nose nervously. "I'd say she's right."

It was the cheesiest line she'd ever heard a boy say to anyone in real life. It would be cheesy for a Disney teen drama show. But she could tell that he'd worked on it for quite a while, so it wouldn't do to laugh at him. "Oh, that's so sweet."

"You know," Hunter said, "now that we're alone, I wanted to tell—"

"I got one!" Kelton shouted from behind them on the big rock.

Now Annette did laugh. Hunter's timing was terrible.

"Well, almost alone," Hunter said. "I wanted to talk to you about the dance last night. I know I didn't get the chance to talk to you, er, you know, because I was going to ask you to dance. If you wanted, I mean. But, see, I was going to ask you, but then—"

Annette's line jerked and her rod bent. An instant later, so did Hunter's.

Why? A slow biting day, and we hardly talk that whole time.

Then, as soon as Hunter's about to say something, we both get a bite? "Two at a time!" Annette said.

"It's not possible that we both caught the *same* one, is it?" Hunter asked. "I mean, the bites came at almost the exact same moment."

As if in answer to his question, two separate scrambling splashes broke the surface. Annette's rod bent more, curved way down. "I must have a big one!"

"It's gonna bust your pole," Hunter said. "Can you bring that in?"

"Yeah, I got it," Annette snapped. The doubt in his voice was annoying, like he didn't think she knew what she was doing. She'd fished so much more than him. "He's got some fight in him. Going to work him, wear him down." She let out some line, reeled some in, trying to exhaust him.

Hunter fought for his fish too. "It's not that. Just that I think you've snagged a real big one. I'm gonna cut mine loose, help you with yours."

"Hunter, no!" Annette shouted. "The bet! We need them both. Anyway, there's not much you can do to help me."

"I'll grab the line, help you bring it in."

Annette released some line. When she pulled her rod back, she felt some tension slackening. "Hunter, if you do that, I'll lose the natural variable resistance, all the give-and-take in my arms and in the rod. You'll make it more likely the line will break."

"Right." Hunter worked his fish. "So, we're on our own."

Annette smiled at him. "Just with the fishing." *Where did that come from?* The fish gave a hard tug. She loved this part, the thrill of it, the excitement, wondering if she'd succeed or if the fish would get away. "Come on, buddy," she said to the fish. "You can't get away. I've got you."

Hunter hauled his fish up, a solid trout. He pulled the hook out and tried to set the fish down on the wood planks of the bridge, but the slippery fish flipped about. Hunter looked ridiculous, reaching for the scale with one hand and making an effort to control his fish with the other, but in the next instant, the fished flopped right off the bridge and splashed down to the water below. He held up shaking fists. "Curse you, Mr. Fish!"

Annette laughed. "No, don't make me laugh. This is hard enough. It's too big to just pull up." It was a struggle, but Annette managed to keep control of the rod while making it off the bridge to the riverbank. There, she hauled the fish in, slipped a couple of fingers into its gills, and yanked it out of the water. "Oh wow!" Annette couldn't contain her excitement. "Look at this thing!" She held it in both hands. With Hunter's help, she soon had it on the scale. Twelve pounds!

"Annette!" Swann shouted from over on her rock as Annette showed off her catch. "This is the biggest one yet! The others won't catch anything like this! You might have won it for us!"

Hunter took a picture before she lowered the fish back toward the river. She looked at the huge fish before she dropped it into the water with a satisfying splash. The biggest she'd ever caught. Incredible. She watched the fish hurry off through the clear river water before she and Hunter exchanged smiles. She was breathing heavy, her heart pounding.

Once, a few years ago, Annette had heard someone blathering at school about how fishing was just a lot of waiting around. But if that guy had felt this excitement and surge of adrenaline, from the first nibble to the capture of the biggest, toughest fish, he'd know what real fun, what a real rush, this sport could be.

Annette closed her eyes and lay back across the footbridge, resting in the hot sun. A shadow fell across her. She opened her eyes, squinting up at Swann, who stood smiling down at her.

"It seems like such a waste to catch these fish, just to let them go."

"Well, if we had brought some buckets or a cooler, we could take some back," Annette said.

"Do you really know how to, like, turn the fish from a swimming creature into a fillet to eat?" Swann asked.

Annette sat up and opened her eyes, blinking in the brightness. "I've always cleaned the fish with my dad, but I could probably do it on my own."

Swann and Kelton sat down on the bridge. Swann sighed. "It would be so awesome to just catch a meal right out of the river."

Annette loved fish, especially a popping-hot fried fish she'd caught herself. "My favorite fish to eat is walleye, but they bite better in the winter, taste better in winter too. It has to do with the kind of food they're eating." Annette smiled with a memory. "Once my dad nearly brought in a walleye, had to be at least nineteen pounds."

"Nineteen pounds of fish?" Swann said. "That's enormous!"

"Would have made for several great meals," Annette said.

Annette offered a round of sodas, and with them, the group had another snack break. "We really should have planned this better," Annette said. "Brought a whole picnic."

"Yumi's dad has a bunch of Army field rations, the MREs?" Hunter said. "We take them hunting and camping. They're pretty good when you figure they're shelf-stable and don't have to be cooked."

"My mom's ex-boyfriend Steve used to talk about all the great things he would have done in the Army if he had joined. He bought some of those things once. Mine wasn't that great," Kelton said. "But what's the deal with Yumi? She just took off? Did we make her mad somehow?" He lowered his gaze. "I guess maybe we weren't talking to her a super-lot over on the boulder."

Swann patted Kelton's arm. "True, but she could have talked to us too. It's like those memes online that talk about how you might feel bad when you haven't texted or contacted your friends, but then you realize the internet works two ways and nobody has contacted you either."

"I don't think you offended her," Hunter said. "Yumi's just direct. Sometimes people mistake her honesty for her being angry or mean. She'll be fine. I can tell."

"You two are amazing," Swann said. "The way you're so close? I'm not even like that with anybody. I guess I'm close with my parents, closer now after the snowmobile disaster, but it's different with parents, you know? Things change when you're twelve or so."

Annette barely ever had the chance to talk to her parents. Dad worked long hours at the printing company down in Boise. Mom worked at McCall City Hall. Even when they were home, they were tired, plus they had to deal with her sister and three brothers. "Yeah, being out with friends is way different than being with family." She sipped her soda.

"But Hunter and Yumi are both," Swann said, sounding impressed.

"It's not that weird, is it?" Hunter said. "We're about the same age, same grade in school. We've grown up together, so we've always played together or hung out at family Thanksgiving and Christmas. My mom would babysit her. Her mom would babysit me. A lot of growing up together." Hunter smiled. "Like the first time either of us went fishing, first fish I ever caught. This tiny little one, half the length of a dollar bill. But I was scared to touch it."

"Aww, that's so cute," Annette said without thinking. But if she'd embarrassed Hunter, he didn't show it and merely smiled.

"It was slippery and flopping around. I was too scared to touch it, almost going to cry."

Kelton laughed a little. "Dude, seriously?"

Hunter frowned. "Cut me some slack, Kel. I was maybe five years old. But Yumi picked it right up, and even though she said it was yucky or something, she brought it close to her face and started opening and closing her mouth, making a fish face. My dad, Grandpa, and Uncle Rick laughed and laughed." He ripped a strip of beef jerky in half with his teeth and talked with his mouth full. "Grandpa tells that story about every time we go fishing." Hunter paused for a moment, chewing and swallowing his jerky. "Yeah, me and Yumi are friends. She's awesome."

"It's too bad she left," Swann said. Nobody said anything for a long moment. The river gurgled around the rocks below. Kelton crunched a chip. The pines swayed in a wave of strong wind. Hunter slurped a drink of soda. "Thanks for this, you guys." Swann held up her soda in salute.

Annette frowned. "It's just the cheap, generic kind of soda. My parents buy it by the case, and my brothers—"

"Oh, I didn't mean thanks for the soda," Swann said. "Thanks for that, but also, thanks for this trip."

"Fishing is fun." A strong breeze blew Annette's hair in her face and she pushed it out of the way. "Could do without this wind, though."

"Yes, but I mean . . ." Swann was struggling to find the right words, looking uncharacteristically unsure of herself. She continued, "I mean for helping me feel like I belong. For being nice to me."

Was this really happening? How could a girl as rich, beautiful, talented, and sophisticated as Swann ever feel like she didn't belong? As soon as Swann had arrived in McCall, almost all the girls changed their hairstyle and clothes to imitate whatever Swann did. Almost all the guys had crushes on her, acting completely stupid whenever she was around. Annette's locker wasn't far from Swann's, and she'd seen all the notes Swann had been given.

Annette smiled. How could a girl like Swann be grateful for the company of a girl like Annette? But then she thought of the war. It had been bad enough for Annette, with people posting crudely Photoshopped pictures of her and saying all kinds of cruel things online, and all Annette had done was point out how both sides had been mean and how everybody would be better off if a truce were called. Swann had been one of the main targets.

"But besides that group back at Painted Pond, everybody likes you, Swann," said Kelton. "I mean, you were on the cover of *People* magazine! That's so cool."

Swann frowned at him. She looked more bothered by what Kelton had said than when they'd discovered McKenzie's crew had beaten them to their fishing spot.

"I was on the magazine because of my parents. A lot of people want to talk to me because my parents are in movies," Swann said. "They'll come up to me and shout, 'Sliding into destiny,' or 'Things are heating up out here in the snow,' from *Snowtastrophe III*, or—"

"I think the 'Things are heating up' line is from *Snowtastrophe II*," Hunter interrupted.

Swann closed her eyes and let out a long breath. "My point is, none of that is me. People think they want to be with me, but they're just excited about famous stuff or whatever. They don't want to spend time with me or get to know *me*." She gestured around them. "That's why I love the woods. Nobody asking for my autograph out here."

"Swann?" Kelton said. "Can I have your auto—"

"I will push you off this bridge," Swann said. "I'm trying to be serious. Thanks for, you know, being with *me*."

Annette cast her lure out into the river. "That's what I've been trying to say. One of the best things about fishing is getting away from the world. Just us, nature, and the challenge of catching fish."

They all went back to fishing from the bridge for a while.

THE FIRE WAS A LARGE LIVING THING, LIKE AN ANIMAL, breathing with a sinister hiss as it stalked through the woods. And the creature was hungry. It had a taste for the dry pine cones and needles, for twigs and branches that had snapped off under the winter's heavy snow and then dried all through the rainless summer. But the monster was never satiated. The more it consumed, the more it wanted, needed to consume.

The wind blew hard, and the fire rushed ahead, flying in white-hot flares of destruction. Tree limbs crackled and crunched as it bit down in flame. A fallen tree trunk exploded in the heat, sending hot chunks of wood flying out into new dry places where the fire could spawn and spread out until it all united. Flames raced up standing trunks almost as fast as water would have rushed down them. Only there was no water. Day after day, week after week, the blazing-hot sun had shone down from cloudless skies that now hung heavy and brown every day. The sun shined through, an angry red orb, matching the orange flames.

The ring of fire spread along the forest floor faster and faster in the wind. It neared a trash bag that had blown out of the back of a passing pickup that winter. The bag swelled, melted, bubbled, and burned in an instant, newspaper, a cardboard milk carton, and Christmas wrapping paper blackened at the edges, flames dancing over them. And when the wind blew, the burning papers rose and scattered, some flying up over the shrubs, over the hill to dry undergrowth on the other side. Some burning papers lodged in the needles of the pines overhead. The greener needles took longer to ignite, giving up their last moisture in sizzling protest.

But it was a hot day, hotter near the fire, and so very dry. At last small fireballs burst up in the branches, the flames crackling and scrambling higher and higher in the trees. Burning chunks of wood fell to the ground below and the fire grew and grew.

An old enormous pine at the top of the hill, its trunk three feet thick, had finally succumbed to the endless onslaught of the wood beetles and died last spring. Winter winds had pushed it into a precarious lean. When the flames found its delicious dry bark and half of the trunk exposed with no protection, they blazed fiercely, devouring the tree so that it quickly flared like a colossal match head, and minutes later finally gave up the struggle to stand. When the burning tree slammed into the ground with a crackling crunch, fire burst out in a circle all around it.

The fire took mere seconds to bite into the shrubs and pine debris all about, pausing as if to savor the new food, before reaching out again for more and more. Pure white-hot flame swirled and roared, rejoicing in its destructive dance across two hills. It grew stronger, spread faster, burned hotter, and raged, hungrier and hungrier to consume, to burn everything it could possibly touch.

CHAPTER 7

AT THE TOP OF THE RIDGE OVERLOOKING THE VALLEY IN which her friends were fishing, Yumi paused to look back. There they were, having a great time, two by two, without her. She had told them all to stay, said she'd be fine, and she would be fine. She thought about Annette in particular. Why couldn't they get their friendship back to the way it used to be? Annette had barely tried to persuade Yumi to stay. Worse, Hunter had made even less of an effort.

Oh no. Am I being a drama queen?

Yumi took a deep breath and turned away from her friends down on the bridge, her footfalls crunching on beds of dry pine needles. She would not be one of these crybabies who always made a big deal out of everything. Morgan Vaughn was the worst of them. She could never seem to get through a school day without crying and making a giant dramatic issue out of something. She'd sit with Swann at lunch, and then cry because she hadn't sat with McKenzie. The next day, she'd sit with McKenzie and then cry because she'd left out Swann. Yumi had wanted to grab the girl by the shoulders and shake her, like, *It's just lunch! It's not that important. Almost nothing is that important. Pick a table and sit down to eat.*

"Make a decision and stick with it," Yumi said aloud, in part wishing Morgan could hear her, but more to herself. She had decided to leave. Annette and Hunter hadn't told her to go. She was pathetic to be sad because none of them had thrown a big enough fit over her decision to leave. What did she expect? That the four of them would be down on their knees, hands pressed over their hearts or held together as if in prayer, crying and begging Yumi to stay? No. Of course that was crazy.

"Enough!" She set off again at a brisk march and would not go back. The top of the ridge was wide, but Yumi crossed it quickly, a few quick steps and a jump up onto the side of an old fallen tree. A jump back down, six fast steps, and she ducked beneath the low branches of a large wilted bush.

Alone and determined, she hurried through the woods and returned to the hill overlooking Painted Pond in much less time than it had taken her group to reach Annette's river fishing spot.

But at the south edge of the top of the ridge she slowed down. For over a week the skies around McCall had been tinged with a faint smoke haze. Nothing too bad. They were stuck in the stage when, if your weather app hadn't told you it was smoke, you might have thought it was a sort of fog. But in the near-distance there was a thicker cloud. Cloud of what? It was the time of year when McCall didn't see a lot of clouds, but they weren't impossible.

Yumi bit her lip. If that gray column was smoke, how close was it? Judging the location of things from a distance was tricky. If that was smoke, it could be ridiculously far away and someone else's problem. And it might not even be smoke. She sniffed deeply, but that was useless. During fire season the air almost always smelled a little smoky.

Should she go back and warn her group? But warn them about what? It might be nothing. If she ruined their happy couples' fishing day over what turned out to be nothing more than a cloud, they'd think she ruined everything because she was the odd person out and felt jealous.

Was she jealous?

The sound of giggle-screams and laughter from down below interrupted her thoughts. She saw them, the other side of the war, down on the crude beach. They'd clearly given up on fishing. McKenzie and Morgan, already soaking wet, acted like they were oh-so-afraid as they tried pushing each other into the water. They were in swimsuits, which they must have worn under their clothes. Had they ever had any intention of fishing at all?

"No!" Morgan squealed. McKenzie had picked her up, baby-cradle-style, and was hobbling out deeper into the pond. "Don't! It's too cold!"

It was late August, temperatures had been in the upper nineties or lower hundreds for over two weeks, and Painted Pond wasn't that deep. There was no way that water was cold.

McKenzie stumbled and both girls laughed and screamed and splashed, flopping around like freshly released fish.

But now that she thought about fish, where was Mason? Yumi shielded her eyes from the hot sun, and finally spotted him on the far side of the pond, arms folded. She couldn't make out his expression very well way up here with the sun beaming down on her, but from his posture she could tell he wasn't happy.

He'd come all the way out here to fish, and these clowns were messing around. He wasn't going to catch anything with the other two stirring up the whole pond.

She glanced at the ominous new cloud again. "Come on, Yumi. Move!" She hurried down the rocky slope toward Painted Pond. "Hey, you guys!" she called out as she neared the bottom.

"Well, look who it is," McKenzie said. "Yooooomee."

McKenzie liked to exaggerate the *You* sound in Yumi's name. Maybe the mean girl thought it would hurt her feelings, trying to make fun of her half-Japanese background? Yumi shrugged. She liked her name. But she said nothing until she'd reached the beach. She pointed south. "Hey, you all see that? Is that smoke?"

"Is what, *what*?" McKenzie laughed, as though mocking Yumi for saying something ridiculous.

What was wrong with these girls? Yumi nodded toward the cloud and spoke extra-loudly and slowly, the way some jerk people did to foreigners or people like Yumi and her mom when they *thought* they were foreigners. "Is. That. Smoke?" She pointed. "O-ver. There?"

"Why do you people have to come ruin our fun?" McKenzie asked. "Where's the rest of your stupid group?"

"They're still fishing," Yumi said. She nodded as Mason

approached, his gear all packed up and an angry scowl on his face. But did his expression lighten when he saw Yumi?

"Who knows what that is, Yumi?" Morgan, who had swum out a few strokes into the pond, finally emerged from the water. "Could be smoke, but it's probably hundreds of miles away in, like, Montana or someplace."

"Yeah. Like, for sure," Yumi said with a big fake smile. "Except that's like south, not east, so unless Montana picked itself up and moved to Utah, that cloud is, like, totally not coming from Montana."

"OK, Geography Jones!" Morgan flipped water out of her hair.

"Are you kidding me?" Mason snapped. "This could be serious, and you're making fun of her? Just because she knows directions and where the states are?"

Yumi and Mason exchanged a brief look, and in that moment Yumi felt something she'd never experienced before. A tightness in her chest, but not from pain. A little tingle went up the back of her neck. Why? Because this guy had agreed with her and defended her? First of all, she, Yumi Higgins, space warrior princess tougher than any she'd read about in her manga books and daughter of an American Army combat veteran, did *not* need anyone speaking for her or defending her. Second, why should she care what this boy thought? She didn't care. Just because he was the best fisher in the school and one of the best in a big-time outdoor sports town like McCall, and his eyes were an almost supernatural deep blue. She squeezed the handle of her fishing pole. She didn't want to be like the girls in those fake fairy-tale love-story romance books. *Then* why *am I thinking about this now?*

"We need to go check out what's going on," Yumi said.

"It's not even that smoky out here," McKenzie said. "It's been a lot smokier when the fire was nowhere near McCall. So if it's hardly smoky at all, whatever you *think* you've seen must be forever away. Sorry, Yuuuumee. You're not going to ruin our awesome day."

Mason glanced at McKenzie and shook his head. To Yumi he said, "You ready?"

"Yeah." Yumi took off down the rough trail toward the Gator.

"Oh come on, Mason!" McKenzie called after them. "Don't leave us! We were having fun!"

Yumi ignored them, moving as fast as she could through the woods. She took a sip from her drinking tube. Hiking could be hard work. It was a lot harder when she was trying to move quickly. Once she stopped to look back and check on Mason. He was three paces behind her. When he smiled he had this dimple and Yumi turned away at once.

"I'm right with you, Yumi," Mason said. "I don't know what's wrong with those two back there. McKenzie came up to me at the dance, said she and Morgan and some others were going fishing and would I like to go along."

"Naturally you said yes, because you're a fishing pro," Yumi said. She tripped over a rock and might have fallen, but Mason quickly dropped his fishing pole and seized her arm to prevent her from going down.

"Thanks," she said, feeling stupid for stumbling and feeling the press of his fingers on her arm long after he'd let her go.

"The others McKenzie had hinted about either backed out or were never really invited, because it was just those two girls and me, catching a ride from McKenzie's older sister and then walking forever. All that way and they hardly cared about fishing. The worst part was they took up the old debate about if fishing is really a sport, going on about how fishing can't count as a real sport because there is no competition, no winners or losers. But anyone who says that hasn't faced the challenge of figuring out how to catch a champion-weight bass. If you ask me, fishing is more of a sport than anything at school."

"Oh yeah," Yumi agreed. "But do you see, they've caught you just like you've hooked a largemouth bass."

"What?" Mason said.

"We've all been taught to worship sports, as if they are the best things in life and the highest praise for something is calling it a sport. That's crazy. You love fishing. I love video games. Swann has this great library, I guess, and she loves reading. Annette lives to write. Sports are no better than anything else, and if you look at the way some of the athletes in our school act, sometimes sports make things a lot worse. Why should we care if people call things sports or not?"

Mason was quiet for a while. Yumi could hear the crunch and scrape of his shoes on the dry pine needles and loose rocks.

Had she offended him? Was he mad because he thought that she didn't consider fishing a sport? Not for the first time that day, she told herself that she didn't care what Mason Bridger thought.

"You're right," he said slowly. He let out a short little laugh. "Who cares if something gets called a sport?"

The forest began to thin out as they approached the wide rough clearing where, earlier that morning, Annette had parked the Gator. The two of them quieted down, noticing the sound of crackling and popping. The smoke—there was no denying now that it *was* smoke—was much thicker. Yumi blinked against the sting. They summited a little rise, and a wave of heat pushed against them, more intense even than the blast one felt when opening a hot oven. The trees on the far side of the wide clearing roared with fire. One with a small-diameter trunk snapped in half and crashed to the burning forest floor. The fire blazed in a slowly but steadily advancing ring of white-red flame. Fire slithered up the trunks of one tree after another, the needles at the tops seeming to explode all at once before the fire even touched them.

The John Deere Gator was parked at least a full thirty feet from the wall of fire. But its bright yellow foam seats darkened like toasted marshmallows. Then they bubbled and finally burst into flame, and in seconds the entire machine burned.

"There goes our ride," Yumi whispered. Her legs felt weak, shaking. "What are we gonna do? Should we backtrack to warn the others, or should we go back to town and get help? But how could we even get to McCall? I guess we could cut over to the right. No fire over there. Head west to get around it and then keep going south."

Mason pulled her down into a crouch where the air was a tiny bit cooler and less smoky. A very tiny bit. He pointed to the top of the low ridge over in the area Yumi said they might go. "See the smoke? The wavy heat lines? It's burning on the other side of that rise. We go over there to get around this, we'll run right into the fire and then this could spread behind us and we'd be trapped."

Yumi whipped out her phone. "We're closer to town." But there was no signal. She shook her head. Mason tried his without success. "Out of range. Why do we have to live in the last place in America with no cell service?" Yumi slipped her phone back in her pocket. "The fire's between us and home. We're cut off. We can't go around it, and we definitely can't stay here. That leaves just one option."

"We go north," Mason agreed.

Yumi nodded. "Let's get the others and find a way to safety."

Mason snapped a photo of the inferno. "They better believe us now."

Yumi put her hand on Mason's shoulder, surprised to find it so firm. She could feel the muscle there. It must have been from all that arm work fishing. *Stop it, Yumi!* "Remember how we were talking about sports?"

"I don't think now's really the time to be worrying about—"

She forced a smile through her terror. "You ever think about going out for track?"

Mason shrugged. "We'll be track stars today!"

They took off running. After a hundred yards or so they were both breathing heavy and coughing from the smoke, but they kept moving as fast as they could, running for their lives, and for the lives of their friends.

Sheriff Hank Hamlin sat in the front of his cop SUV, parked south of town in a little lot with trees all about, waiting to catch some speeders coming into McCall. He closed his eyes as he cracked open an ice-cold can of Mountain Dew. *If you're tired and need a boost, get a cup of coffee*, his wife Emily always said. She didn't want him drinking all the corn syrup. But the one thing she couldn't seem to understand was that the soda wasn't about waking him up. He'd already stopped by Sharlie's Coffee Shop when he'd started his shift. His midday Mountain Dew was all about the flavor. "Anyway, Emily," he said quietly, as if she could hear, "I hardly ever have these anymore. It's been a tough week."

He always felt bad parked with the engine idling, wasting the county's fuel, so the truck and its air conditioner were shut off. He pressed the cool can to his face in the heat. It had been a rough week. Not one, but two fights at the Bear Stone Brewery. Drunken tourists. A kid nearly drowned in the lake. This was his last day on the job before a week's vacation. The family was heading down to California to visit the big mouse. The kids were getting a little too old for some of that princess stuff, but they'd asked for Disneyland for years. It would cost a fortune, but Emily reminded him the kids were growing up and would be moving out sooner than he thought. So Disney. Legoland. Maybe he'd make a fool of himself and try surfing. Family time. It would be good.

"About five hours to go," he said quietly.

A guy in a slick yellow Dodge Challenger with a black racing stripe zipped by doing fifty-four in a thirty. Hank started his truck and flipped on his lights. "OK, Dale Earnhardt. Let's get you stopped before you hit some kid walking with an ice-cream cone." He pulled out of the lot onto Highway 55, heading north.

Deputy Abrams came on the radio. "*Sheriff Hamlin, this is dispatch.*"

Bad timing. He radioed back. "Hank here. Go ahead, over."

"*Smoke spotted north of the lake. Eastside Drive. Got a report it's bad. Fire's on its way. Forest Service notified.*"

Sheriff Hamlin sighed and radioed back. "Darn it, Jaylen. Didn't I say no fires, no missing persons, no nothing? I'm almost on vacation." He sped up. The racer in the Challenger pulled over. Hank squawked the sirens and pointed at the guy. "Ease off the gas, high-speed." The guy in the Dodge couldn't hear him, but he hung his head, getting the message.

Hank radioed dispatch. "Jaylen, Hank. What are the odds this is just a nice easy little ditch fire we'll have out in—" He reached a more open spot on the highway, free of trees and buildings. He had a better view north. The column of smoke rising up there was thick and dark. Hank cursed, keeping the mike keyed. He wanted to believe this was nothing, but with twenty-three years in Idaho law enforcement, this was certainly not his first fire season. He cursed again. "Jaylen, could you call my wife? Tell her the vacation's probably postponed."

"You got it, boss."

Hank fired up the siren and hammered on the gas to hurry north through town as fast as he safely could. Two fights, a near-drowning, and now a fire. This was a bad, bad week.

Yumi could hardly breathe by the time she and Mason returned to Painted Pond. It had been hard to run that far, and even worse running with her fishing pole and thermos. They jogged to a halt on the beach, both of them panting and coughing.

"What's up with you two?" McKenzie said, sitting up from where she and Morgan had been sunbathing on towels. Some of the edge in her usual mocking tone was gone.

Morgan rolled onto her side. She looked worried. "Did you figure out what's going on?"

"Well, that smoke's not coming from MontanUtah," Yumi said sharply. It was stupid to be bitter, and they didn't have time for snarky remarks, but those two had been mean and, worse, they'd wasted a lot of time.

Mason was more efficient. He put his fishing gear down and held up his phone, showing the picture of the blaze. "Fire. A big one. Wind's blowing it right for us. We gotta get out of here." He coughed and spit.

"Did you call for help?" Morgan asked feebly. Anyone on her phone as much as Morgan knew they had no signal out here. Yumi and Mason ignored the question.

"Well, you ran all the way here," McKenzie said. "It's way back there, right? We have time."

"No!" Mason shouted. "With this wind, the fire will spread fast. How fast do you think we ran?"

"And not all of that running was in a direction away from the fire," Yumi said. "Anyway, you think they issue evacuation orders to people who live near a burning because the fire moves slowly and gives everybody plenty of time?"

Morgan pointed to the pond. "Let's just get in the water. The fire won't be able to touch us."

Mason was usually a quiet, mild kind of a guy. When he shouted a curse, it made everybody jump. "Think about it! Fire doesn't just destroy all the wood, grass, and *people* in its path. It also consumes oxygen. Even *if* the fire doesn't eat all the oxygen and suffocate us, you don't understand that level of heat. The flames weren't even near Annette's Gator, and the seats started burning. Now with these trees all around right up to the water's edge, imagine that kind of heat searing our faces when we surface to try to breathe."

"Plus the smoke," Yumi said. "It would choke us out."

"Soon nothing will be able to survive here," Mason said.

McKenzie and Morgan dropped their usual sarcastic know-it-all attitudes. McKenzie clapped her hands, as if she were the queen, deciding for everyone. "OK, let's get dressed and get out of here."

"Maybe we should keep wearing our wet clothes," Morgan said. "Fire doesn't like water, right? The water in our swimsuits could protect us from sparks. Keep us cool if we're too close to the heat."

"Hurry up and change your clothes," Mason said. "My dad helps fight forest fires. Tells me all about it. Wet clothes around fires this hot are the worst. The water in the fabric won't protect you. It will boil into steam and burn your flesh."

The girls went behind a boulder to change. When they returned, Morgan was shaking so bad, Yumi worried she'd collapse.

"Calm down," McKenzie snapped. "You make it, like, ten times worse freaking out about it."

Yumi was about to shout at McKenzie, to tell her to try not to be such an evil witch. But that would just start a fight and make things worse.

"It's bad," Yumi said. "I won't lie. But we're ahead of it. We'll keep moving. Find the others and get help."

They hurried to the steep painted-rock slope. "We have a lot of ground to cover," Yumi said. She tossed her fishing pole and thermos aside. The latter might have been good for hauling drinking water, but she'd have to get by with just her CamelBak, and anyway she needed both hands. "Our stuff will slow us down. Ditch anything you don't absolutely need."

McKenzie and Morgan put their fishing poles on the ground. After a moment, they dropped the swimsuits they'd been carrying. Mason sighed and gave up his tackle box. He was about to do the same with his fishing rod, but shook his head.

"Seriously?" Yumi asked.

Mason stood firm. "This is my lucky fishing pole. It's top-of-the-line. It goes with me."

"I will buy you a new pole, Mason!" McKenzie snapped. "Drop it, so we can go faster!"

"It's fine!" Yumi said. "Let's go!"

The group started the climb, easy at first, but then troubling them with some big boulders. Yumi found her way to the top of one and offered her help to Morgan, who accepted. When she pulled Morgan up, the two of them stood close for a moment. Yumi could feel the girl shaking. She patted Morgan's shoulder. "We'll be OK," Yumi said quietly. "I know the way. We'll keep moving and be fine."

After a tough scramble up the first slope, the group paused at the top of the hill, looking back toward McCall. Between them and home, a darker, angrier column of smoke rose from the wilderness.

"It's getting worse," Yumi said. She might have sounded calm and confident to the others, but she didn't feel it. Her legs shook and she wanted to throw up. The quick exchange of a look with Mason told her he felt the same way, and somehow his fear helped her feel less alone.

"Fire can spread fast," Mason said. "Thick forest? Maybe six miles per hour. More open, grassy land? Maybe fourteen miles per hour."

Morgan threw a stone over the edge of the rocky slope they'd just climbed. It clicked as it bounced down. "What's our top running speed? *Maybe* twenty miles per hour?"

"Not even close to that speed, especially through this terrain," Mason said.

"I won't lie to you. We're in a lot of trouble. We have to move. Fast." Yumi took a deep breath. She stepped close to Mason and whispered, "Will you bring up the rear? Help out if anyone falls? Keep them moving?" Mason nodded. To the others, Yumi spoke with as much confidence as she could muster. "Now we run. No stopping. Follow me."

Yumi took off running, risking tripping over a rock or branch when she briefly turned to look back and make sure the others were following. Yumi had participated in McCall's youth running club before, tackling runs up to three miles. The distance they had to cover to reach Hunter and the others wasn't as far, but this would still be the longest run of their lives.

CHAPTER 8

"YUMI, HOW BAD IS IT?" SWANN ASKED.

Yumi was still bent over, hands on her knees, trying to get her breath back after the long run, and coughing. She was drenched in sweat now, dirt smudged across her forehead.

"It's . . ." Yumi coughed hard, tears in her eyes. "It's bad. Getting worse."

Swann tapped at her phone. "No service, so, we need to go for help."

McKenzie managed to straighten herself up and put a hand on her hip. "Come on, Swann. You've known about the fire for about thirty seconds. Don't act like you're taking over. You're not in charge of everything."

"Oh, I'm sorry, McKenzie. Maybe you would rather hang around and get burned up. It's not taking over to suggest we don't die."

"Stop it!" Annette shouted. "Both of you! Nobody is in charge! That's so stupid. It doesn't matter. All that matters is surviving. First we need to know what we're dealing with. Yumi, tell us what's up."

Yumi and Mason explained how'd they'd seen the smoke and tried to head back home, but were blocked by the fire.

"And I'm sorry, Annette, but the Gator is history," Yumi said. "We watched it burn."

Annette blew out a breath. "Even if I survive the fire, my parents are going to kill me."

"Then we have to run," Hunter said. "No choice, right?"

Morgan waved her hands in front of her chest. "We gotta rest a little bit. Been running forever."

"What we really need to do is call for help," Annette said. She took a deep breath, hoping she had the right idea.

"Yeah, that's great, dummy, except our phones won't work out here," McKenzie said.

Yumi scowled. "What is *wrong* with you?"

McKenzie held up her phone and was about to say something.

"Enough!" Annette shouted, with more confidence than she felt. "We don't have time to fight. There's a cabin. It might have an old telephone, like that one with the loud bell that Yumi and Hunter have on the wall at their hunting lodge. Let's go." She didn't wait for the others but ran across the bridge over the river and onto the gravel foot trail beyond. The trail rose at a gentle slope around a little hill. At the top she glanced back, relieved to see the others were following.

A minute later, a red-painted A-frame cabin came into view,

a wooden picnic table and a couple of Adirondack chairs out front. Reaching the place, Annette tried the front door. Locked.

"What do we do now?" Morgan asked nervously.

"Do we even have time for this?" McKenzie added. "Maybe we should keep running? Or trying to run."

"Maybe there's a key?" Hunter said.

Annette looked for a key, hanging from a nail on the door trim or under a welcome mat. There wasn't a welcome mat.

Idaho didn't always get a lot of rain in the summer, but the state always had tons of rocks. Annette picked up a softball-sized stone and bashed in the front window beside the door, jerking her hand back as sharp shards of glass fell.

"You could have warned us," Yumi said.

"You're the one who's gotta pay for that, Annette," McKenzie said.

Annette used the rock to smash out the few jagged pieces of glass that remained in the frame.

"Or else this whole cabin will be burned down and nobody will care about a window," Hunter countered.

"If it *doesn't* burn, someone will want to know who broke this window, and I *will* tell—"

"They can bill *me*, McKenzie!" Swann shouted. "Shut up!"

Yumi and Hunter moved together without speaking, dragging one of the chairs to the wall.

"You're the coolest, Annette." Yumi stepped on the chair, then on the window frame, before jumping down into the cabin. A moment later the door was unlocked and swung open.

Everybody rushed in, almost as if they thought being in the cabin would somehow shield them from the coming fire.

The ground floor of the cabin was a simple single room. There was an ancient plaid sofa and worn recliner near the front facing a black cast-iron woodstove. The beds, if there were any, must have been upstairs. At the far end of the rectangular room was a kitchen area with a refrigerator, sink, cabinets, and table. There, on the wall beside the fridge, was a big yellow telephone, a holdover relic from the 1900s.

"Bingo," Annette said, flipping on the lights and rushing to the phone. "We have power. Now let's just hope this old . . ." She yanked the heavy handset and held it to her ear. Silence. ". . . old piece of *junk* works. It doesn't." Her shoulders slumped. She'd wasted precious time leading them to this stupid cabin. All for a dead phone.

"You didn't even turn it on." Morgan flopped down on the sofa, making a dusty cloud. "Is there a button you have to push to make a call? Like an old-time send button?"

McKenzie pointed at the phone. "It has to be that giant claw thing the handle was hanging on. You press that or something."

Annette moved the claw up and down. Nothing. She looked the phone over carefully. "There's a loudness dial. Nothing else."

"Give me that." Yumi snatched the handset away from her. She held it to her ear for a moment before slamming it back onto its wall mount. "Phone's dead," Yumi said decisively. "My grandpa has one of these at the lodge. You pick it up, and it should start making this sort of buzzing noise. This isn't."

"Great." McKenzie threw her hands up, pacing the room, her shoes crunching over broken glass. "Well, this was a pointless waste of time that we don't have. Thanks a lot, Annette."

"You don't like it, you can take off, McKenzie," Yumi shouted. "Nobody's stopping you. Nobody wants—"

"Nobody's splitting up," Annette said. Visions of funerals for her dead classmates, even for those she didn't like that much, flashed through her mind. That would not happen. It couldn't. At least she would do all she could to prevent it. "We're staying together, and we'll make it out of this." She exchanged a doubtful look with Yumi. "We should prepare to be out in the woods for a while."

"What do you mean?" Morgan asked. "Like camping?"

"No shortage of campfires," Kelton said quietly.

"Kelton!" McKenzie began in that snotty way she had of tearing everybody down. But she stopped herself, and then laughed. It was like popping the top on a shaken can of soda. Everybody burst out laughing.

"Anybody got any marshmallows?" Swann asked.

"Yeah," McKenzie added. "And a fire poker that's, like, two miles long."

Annette didn't know much about how to survive a horrible forest fire, but she was trying to be a journalist, a reporter, a writer. So she tried to understand people. And these people all around her needed that break in the tension. They all laughed harder than the jokes merited, and it was good.

"Seriously, though." McKenzie looked out through the glassless window. "What do we do now?"

"We have to keep moving," said Hunter.

"First, we rob this cabin of everything we'll need out there," Kelton said.

Morgan leaned back on the sofa, her hands over her face. "What? Just steal stuff? It's bad enough we broke the window."

"Like I said—" Swann began.

"Yes, we all know you're rich enough to buy this whole cabin, Swann," Morgan said. "But it's wrong. We can't just steal."

"There's real good odds this whole cabin is going to burn to the ground." Hunter threw open the refrigerator door and checked inside. "If I owned this place, I'd be happy that people used whatever they could before it all burned."

It was as if everybody silently agreed at the same time. They all snapped to work. Cabinets were thrown open, a team went upstairs.

In the end, they did not find much. A hatchet. A flashlight. Three shotgun shells, useless without a gun. They found a twenty-four-foot length of rope. Upstairs there were blankets and a few towels. These were about to be discarded, but Hunter and Kelton insisted they take them, along with four old wooden tent stakes, each about a foot long.

Hunter rubbed his leg. "In case we end up having to make another splint. We'll do it right this time."

"Jackpot!" Kelton said, pulling up a panel on the floor and reaching down into the storage space he found there. He produced two enormous metal cans, the kind Annette had seen once on a survival preparation advertisement online. "Hope everybody's hungry, because it looks like . . ." He read the cans. "Like beans and . . . chocolate pudding. Five pounds each." Kelton flipped some buckles on a flat metal tub he found in the storage hatch. He smiled. "Plus"—he held up the prize from the tub—"two sleeves of saltine crackers."

"Are you kidding?" Swann made a disgusted grunt. McKenzie was about to pounce, but Swann continued, "No lobster? No caviar? What's the matter with you Idaho people?"

Everybody laughed again.

"Right, Hollywood," Yumi joked. "I'm sure you'll leave a negative review for the manager." To the others she shouted, "If we're going to be eating a bunch of beans somebody go to the outhouse! Grab all the toilet paper."

After they'd packed it all up, cramming it into each of the four backpacks they'd brought, Annette's own, Hunter's, Kelton's, and Swann's, they cranked the handle on the pump until water gushed from the well down a little spout, rust-orange at first, but quickly clearing. Each of them drank and drank. Hunter, Yumi, and Kelton topped off their CamelBak water systems.

While the rest of them drank, Annette spread out the real prize she'd found in the cabin. A paper map of Idaho. Better than a simple road map, this topographical map displayed contour lines to denote elevation and give a better sense of the terrain. It was from the year 1997, but she figured the roads and highways hadn't changed that much since then. The mountains and other terrain made drastic road changes difficult. It wasn't like a north-south freeway had been built in the years since the map was made.

They'd found an old radio upstairs, and they brought it down and plugged it in. Kelton turned it on. "Maybe I can find some news." Static hissed as Kelton turned a dial, trying to tune in a station. *"Idaho's number one country . . ."* He cranked the tuning dial more. *". . . for incredible prices on mattresses, before the sale ends on . . . let it be . . . of the serious situation developing north of McCall."* Kelton shouted, "Hey, quiet, everybody! Listen to this!" He turned up the volume. *"High winds have grounded firefighting aircraft and are making a bad fire situation worse. Warren Wagon Road is closed to all but emergency traffic, so at this time the only open route north out of McCall is the regular Highway 55–95 corridor or up Lick Creek Road to the east. Again, fire crews are responding to a serious wildfire situation north of the city of McCall, Idaho. Residents are advised that, at this time, no evacuation orders have been issued for city residents."*

"We've lost time here," Hunter said, peering over Annette's shoulder at the map. He was standing kind of close. Not too close, but pretty close. She could feel his presence, smell the spice of the jerky he'd eaten earlier. Annette squeezed the edges of the map, wishing she could stop thinking about things that didn't matter right now.

"What do you think?" Annette asked. "Back over the river, and then north? Run from the fire?"

Hunter nodded. "The way the wind's blowing, the fire will head right this way."

Yumi tapped the map. "Radio sounds like we'll never get home by the road. There's no choice. We hook up with Warren Wagon Road and keep going north, trying to hitch a ride or find some way to call for help. At this point, we just keep moving, no matter what. Good plan?"

"Well, none of this is good," Hunter said. She turned to face him, annoyed, but found him smiling. "But for now, it's the best we can do."

"Great, so let's stop yapping about it, and *go!*" Yumi hoisted her drinking pack up on her shoulders and pulled two little straps to tighten the main harness. She had her compass at the ready. "We're moving out!" she yelled to everyone, circling her hand in the air above her head. "Back over the bridge, then north, as fast as we can move." Yumi led off in a jog. Annette followed, Hunter running beside her.

"Thanks for the help," Annette said quietly, wishing she could talk to whomever owned this cabin. "I hope it will be enough."

All eight of them rushed back along the trail and across the bridge over the beautiful swift river. Annette surveyed her favorite fishing spot, this peaceful outdoor paradise where, less than an hour ago, her biggest concern had been talking to Hunter, trying to figure out if he liked her and whether or not she should let him know she liked him. She thought the situation over as the suspension bridge bobbed a little under the footfalls of the larger group. How silly it all sounded, spending so much time and energy worried about crushes when they were in so much danger.

They'd just sat there, joking, fishing, and relaxing in the sun, and all the while a deadly fire was spreading and cutting them off from home. Why hadn't they simply done the easy thing and fished on Payette Lake? Then they'd be safe and comfortable in McCall, probably swimming or eating ice cream by now. Instead, she just had to show off, trying to act like a big expert fisher who knew the woods. She was the one who'd suggested they go fishing way out on Painted Pond. The other group had overheard her and beat them to the place, but after finding their intended fishing spot occupied, did she make the sensible suggestion to just go back? Of course not! She'd dragged them deeper into the wilderness, deeper into trouble. Expert fisher? She didn't know anything.

After crossing the bridge, Yumi pointed with her whole arm, fingers together and extended in this Army gesture her dad sometimes used. She called it "blade hand." In her other hand she held her compass. "We gotta head north. Let's pick up the pace."

The group hurried into a trot, about as fast as they could manage through the thick woods, through the abundant dry fuel for the fire that was coming. All the shrubbery forced them to move in a single-file line or sometimes two-by-two. Morgan and McKenzie stayed close, whispering together, probably more mean cutting comments, probably about Annette and how she'd landed them all in deadly danger.

"I'm really sorry about this, everybody." Annette spoke loudly, so the entire spread-out group could hear. "I didn't mean to trap us all in trouble."

Swann laughed. So did Kelton. They'd stuck close together on this march too.

"What is possibly funny about this, Swann?" McKenzie called out from where she, Morgan, and Mason brought up the rear.

Not the fighting again? Why couldn't everybody leave the war behind? Was it too much to ask that they peace it out long enough for them to return to safety? Should she say something, speak up and ask for calm before another battle ignited?

But Swann did not take the bait. "Oh, sorry," she said. "No, you're right. This is all terrible, but I was just thinking about how when Hunter, Kelton, and I were trapped in the snow up on Storm Mountain, we all kept blaming ourselves."

"Well, I shouldn't have taken that shortcut," Kelton said.

Swann gently bumped her shoulder against Kelton. "If you hadn't, then we wouldn't have spent so much time together in that abandoned mine."

"Yeah, Swann," Hunter said, panting a little as Yumi led them up a rocky slope. They had to watch where they walked, stepping from the top of one rock to another, forcing careful but rapid progress up the hill. "That was really fun. My broken leg and everything."

"You're right," Kelton said. "It was miserable. Just like this has become, but for how it all turned out, I'm glad it happened. And it gives me hope that someday we'll look back on this and be happy about how it ended. For real."

"Oh, that is just so, so cute," McKenzie said. "I'm glad you think this is all a game, Kelton, but some of us are taking this seriously."

"C'mon, McKenzie! I don't think it's a game!" Kelton shouted. "Did I say that? What's the matter with you? You don't think I understand the trouble we're in or what it's like to be stranded out in the wilderness in a dangerous situation?"

"It's OK, Kelton," Swann said quietly. "Let it go."

"I won't let it go!" Kelton shouted. "You may be hot stuff in a fashion show or on the volleyball court, McKenzie, but we're not in school and nobody cares how you look right now. Out here? You're in our world. I used to get all upset when you'd give me crap, used to worry about popularity, the Pops and the Grits. But being out here"—he held his hands wide, gesturing all around—"I figured out that people are people. That's what the wilderness does, strips people down to their basic. I learned that the hard way. I get that. You don't. So let me help you understand something, princess. Nobody's gonna bow to your crown out here. So you can either help us get out of this or quietly accept our help. Either way, shove your oh-so-better-than-everyone attitude, because nobody cares who you think you are."

Annette bit her lip. So much for peacing it out. Kelton had just dropped a gallon of gas on the fire of the war. Annette turned around for a moment to look at him. Who was this guy? It was as if a rebel outsider had gone up on Storm Mountain this last winter and a totally new person had returned. Mrs. Dunlap, their health teacher, had subjected their entire grade to an embarrassing lesson about how they'd all be undergoing significant changes, but she'd said nothing about this kind of total personality transformation.

Mason coughed. Was he covering a laugh? "Smoky out here," he said.

Yumi pressed her fist against her mouth in a halfway effort to hide her laughter. "Some big stones," she said appreciatively. "Big stones up here. Don't trip."

McKenzie had to be mad about Kelton yelling at her. Annette couldn't remember anyone ever talking to her that way. But McKenzie didn't reply. At least not to the whole group. Instead she fell back on her familiar tactic of bitter whispering with Morgan. After more fast hard marching north through the tough terrain, they reached one of those rock features that made the Idaho woods so beautiful, and so challenging. Suddenly great jagged columns of stone rose before them, a barrier that would take forever to climb, assuming they could figure out a way up the nearly vertical slope at all.

Yumi stopped the march and turned back toward the rest of the group. She wiped her forearm over her sweaty forehead. "This is probably as good a place as any to head west to hook up with Warren Wagon Road."

Annette's legs shook like Jell-O. Her muscles ached. The bright blazing afternoon heat cooked her body. She wanted to rest. At the foot of the rise in front of them there were enough big rocks for everyone to sit down for a little time-out. But she didn't dare say anything. She would not be the weak one who first begged for mercy.

The group shifted, like a herd of cattle, without a word, to move west toward the road. Maybe they'd get lucky and find a passing vehicle and they could sit for a ride to safety. On soft seats. With air-conditioning.

After a challenging climb up and down the ridge, it was a short walk through the woods. When they finally stepped out of the scrub brush onto the hot hard blacktop of the road, there was no one and nothing but even more oppressive heat rising in waves off the pavement to cook their legs.

"This isn't the most high-traffic road in the area," Hunter said after a few minutes. "In winter, they just close it to cars and trucks and leave the snow on the road for snowmobiles. Way up north, there are some out-of-the-way bars and restaurants."

"Oh, I wish it was winter," Morgan said quietly.

"I know the radio said the highway's only open to emergency traffic, but someone will probably be driving along soon, though," Kelton said. "Someone like us trying to escape. Probably."

"Maybe." McKenzie cocked a hip out and folded her arms. "But you guys are stupid to hang around talking about it." She started walking north. Morgan glanced around helplessly for a moment before following. When the others joined them, McKenzie led Morgan to the opposite side of the pavement, fast-walking in angry silence.

Swann scoffed and was about to say something, probably something nasty to McKenzie. But Annette held up her hand and the group marched down the road.

CHRIS AND BEN HAD BEEN FRIENDS THEIR WHOLE LIVES, growing up in suburban Portland, Oregon, and graduating from high school together. The summer was nearly over. Soon they'd be off to separate colleges, and as they both acknowledged, they'd probably drift apart.

"But not before we have one last adventure," Chris kept saying. Two weeks ago, the two of them had grabbed whatever camping and hiking gear they could find and crammed it into Ben's mom's minivan. Then they drove off for the middle of nowhere. They'd made it all the way into the deep South Dakota Badlands, taking their time wandering along the most remote roads they could find. Along the way, they saw awesome rodeos, climbed spectacular mountains, and met tons of great people. On their return trip, they drove the van right down by this beautiful crystal-clear creek in the middle of Idaho and spent the day swimming, relaxing, and talking about the future.

That night, Ben had said they shouldn't risk a campfire, but Chris built it right next to the stream, and he kept a bucket of water handy if a spark popped out and started the brush ablaze. Plus he had the tire iron from the van to use as a rake to beat down any fires.

Now, after sleeping late and enjoying one more swim, it was time for the two old friends to roll along, toward the end of their years together, and the start of the journey of the rest of their lives.

"The fire burned all night and no harm done. Down to just hot coals now," Chris said. "See? Nothing to worry about."

Ben pointed to a column of smoke rising in the south. "There's plenty to worry about. People aren't even supposed to have fires in the summer. Make sure you get it all completely out."

Chris held his water bucket up in salute. "No problem." He slowly poured the water from the bucket all around their little fire ring, steam hissing and rising with smoke in a little plume.

When they both saw that their fire was extinguished just as surely as all their other campfires on their adventure had been, they packed their trash and belongings into the van, fired up the engine and music from a special road-trip playlist Ben had made, and rolled off down the highway, heading north toward whatever else they might find.

The firepit remained, sizzling under the hot sun. A sparrow flitted upon a stone on the edge of the circle, chirped, pooped, and flew away. The ashes, washed nearly black by the water from the boys' bucket, slowly brightened to a dark gray, and in the bright sun gradually turned white. An orange glow returned along the underside of the remains of half a log, and a whisp of smoke curled up into the air. The wind blew and more orange blared bright in the remains of the hot wood.

The creek gurgled by and the wind blew and a chipmunk skittered over the rocks searching for seeds for his next meal. Hours passed, and the hot log popped, throwing a red-hot chunk of wood into the tall grass nearby.

The grass did not darken gradually. There was hardly any time for the hot ember to smolder. The wind blew, and fire burst out in the grass, flames climbing the stalks and spreading across the ground, a white-orange ring around a black circle. Pine cones caught and burned just as fast. A bed of pine needles twisted and blackened as the fire raced across them. And within minutes, the fire devoured a large bush, before clambering up into the branches of a pine overhead, and from that pine to the one growing close by. The wind gusted, and the fire roared and spread, releasing its smoke into the air along with a chorus of other blazes across the region. The grasses and undergrowth were high and thick, and the summer had been so very dry, and the fire burned hot, and very, very hungry.

CHAPTER 9

"I DON'T WANT TO SOUND LIKE I'M COMPLAINING. FOR real," said Kelton. He pulled the bottom of his T-shirt up to wipe his sweaty face. Walking on the hard hot pavement in the late afternoon August heat, coupled with the smoke hovering thicker and thicker in the air, punished all of them. "And I know the short answer is basically 'really far,' but how far are we going? What's our plan here? I know eventually this road curves way around the mountains and heads south again."

"He has a point," Annette said. Of course, the most important consideration, at first, was to simply get away from the fire. Who cared about a plan when it was a desperate question of survival? It was still a desperate question of survival. "Obviously we need to keep moving, but it's not like we can walk all the way north to Coeur D'Alene or something."

"There's going to be a bus," Swann said.

"What are you talking about?" Hunter licked his lips, then took a long pull from his drinking tube.

"We're going to find a bus," Swann said. "A real nice one. With a fridge inside it packed with ice water and soda."

"And air-conditioning," Annette added. To get out of this heat, even for a few minutes. To be able to rest without the constant twist of fear deep inside her, to relax and let others take care of everything. "Kelton's right to ask. Where does this end? How do we get out of this?"

Hunter stopped. He leaned over, exhausted, with his hands on his knees. He made a little whimper sound, almost like he was crying. Was he about to collapse?

Without thinking, Annette put her arm over his shoulders. "Hey, you're OK."

"No, I'm not," Hunter said quietly. "We're not. And however we get out of this, it's not this way." He pointed to the north.

Annette's legs nearly gave out. She wanted to drop to the pavement in despair. "Oh no." This couldn't be real. Up ahead, another thick column of dark smoke rose into the sky. "It's not . . . maybe it's just a cloud." She turned around on the road, saw the smoke to the south, and spun back to the north. More smoke. Mountains to the east and west.

"We're trapped?" Swann whispered. "Are we trapped? I mean, what do we do? Where do we go?"

"It's OK," Kelton tried to reassure her. "We'll be all right."

Annette watched the smoke in the north. Standing in the blindingly bright sunlight, it was hard to tell, but she could have sworn she saw a flash, a spark. And above a line of trees, an orange glow. "Is that . . . Look—" Annette pointed toward the glow. "Is that fire? Right there with those trees on that ridge?"

Swann did a kind of stutter step, like she wanted to run, but didn't know which direction. "What do we do?" There was panic in her voice, a loss of control Annette had never witnessed in her before. This was ultra-cool Swann Siddiq. Now there were tears in her wild wide eyes. "Where do we go?"

"Fire to the south," Yumi said. "Fire to the north. That just leaves two directions."

Annette thought about it. "Doesn't east basically lead into endless wilderness?" Yumi nodded. Annette shrugged. "Then we go west."

"What?" McKenzie said, pointing. McKenzie's hair had always been perfect, in the latest fashion, while Annette's own had always been a frizzy mess. Now McKenzie's perfect straight golden hair was a tangled sweat-soaked, dust-crusted nightmare. She sounded as fried as she looked. "Over those mountains?"

Yumi pulled out and unfolded the map. "If we go west, we'll eventually run into Highway 95. That's a more important road. It may still be open."

"Right. This fire can't be everywhere." Hunter tapped the paper in Yumi's hand. "Thank God we found a good map with contour lines to mark elevation. A basic road map would just show this area all green."

Kelton traced his finger along part of the map. "Where the lines are close together means the slope is steeper. Some of these areas the lines are practically touching. That's a cliff."

"The lines are farther apart at that place you're touching," Swann said.

"And it's not so far from where we are," Yumi said. She handed the map to Hunter and took out her compass. "Maybe . . ." She pointed the compass north. "If I had a protractor, I could figure out . . . our exact heading. Which, OK." She was talking mostly to herself, checking the compass, then looking at the map. "If I'm right about where we are on the map right now, and with the compass I can keep our direction consistent. It won't be super-exact because of the difference between north on the map and magnetic north."

"How could there be more than one north?" Morgan asked.

Yumi ignored her. "We'll have to do the best we can navigating by terrain features and rough compass bearing. But I think I can get us up this ravine where the slope isn't as steep. That will get us over one high ridge. Then down through this little valley, and up again over a second ridge, and we can follow this stream, Hazard Creek, as it flows all the way down here near highway 95."

Kelton squinted as he peered at the map. "Well, how do you know it flows to the west?"

Mason shook his head. Swann pressed her fist to her mouth, trying to hide her laughter. Yumi just stared at the guy. "Kel, do you think the water in the creek is flowing *up* the mountain?"

The guy's cheeks flared red. "Oh yeah. Duh. Sorry."

Mason patted his shoulder. "Don't worry about it."

Morgan hadn't been helping much to figure out their route, but she glanced at the map. "But how far is that?"

"It's far." Yumi nodded. "And there's a lot of up and down the mountains. But the straight-line distance isn't much farther than it is from where we are now along this road back to McCall."

"Plus there's no fire on this route through the mountains," Swann said.

"Not that we know of," Morgan replied. Nobody said anything to that.

"We're running out of options," Annette said. "It's this or nothing."

The group slid down the gravelly shoulder off the road, moving west through brown weeds and shrubs. A lot of the terrain surrounding this road was swampy wetlands most of the year. The winter had been very snowy, so the spring runoff from the mountains had been heavy and these lowland areas off the road had flourished with green life. But, after a few cold rain showers early in March, there had been only one or two light sprinkles, not even enough to wet the highway. All eight of them crunched through a dry flat, hurrying toward the high western ridge.

Annette hurried to catch up with Yumi and Hunter, who led the group, Yumi keeping an eye on the compass and map, Hunter whacking down brush with a large stick.

"The wind's mostly blowing north, right?" Morgan said after they'd been walking several minutes. "The fire to the north is closer, but the wind should be pushing it the other direction right?"

"Fire spreads fastest in the direction the wind's blowing, yeah," Mason said. "But it still spreads."

"Oh great," Morgan said. The girl had dropped any pretense at popularity. She was scared. And she was tired. They all were.

"And wind direction can change," Mason said.

"Yep, it's real bad!" McKenzie shouted from the back of the line where she walked with Morgan. "Can we all accept that and just move on? I don't understand why we keep talking doom and gloom. Like, how does that help us?"

The way forward was rough. Hunter helped a little, but Annette still had to pay close attention to where she stepped in order to avoid tripping. Still, she risked turning back to flash a smile at McKenzie, who, Annette had to admit, was right.

But if it made no sense to endlessly repeat how dangerous their situation was, and if the silence only invited more worrying about the same, perhaps what was needed was distraction.

"So, Mason," Annette said. "Mason," she shouted louder to be heard over the crunch of the weeds and the whistle of the wind. "Football practice starts next week. You going to play?"

Mason laughed. "Football? You want to talk about football at a time like this?"

Annette kept her voice light and friendly. "Why not? You have somewhere else you have to be? Something better to do?"

Yumi looked back at her with a confused expression for a moment, but Annette only shrugged.

"Right. Football? Maybe," Mason said. "I think so. I don't know."

"You seem so sure of yourself, Mason," Yumi said.

It was a strange conversation, all of them spread out and

walking single file. They had to practically yell to be heard. "I was joking," Yumi said quickly. "Go on. You were saying you don't know if you're going to play football?"

"Oh, sorry," Mason said. "Yeah, well, I like fishing the most. Wrestling after that. I've been doing OK in the youth wrestling tournaments I've been in. But now, with middle school sports starting, this is the real deal. My cousin down in Boise was a state champion wrestler. He quit football after seventh grade to focus on wrestling. Extra camps. Weight lifting. Running. He didn't want to risk an injury in football that would knock him out of the wrestling season after that."

"You're worried about getting hurt?" Hunter asked. Annette was surprised he had spoken up about it.

"Not hurt," Mason said. "I can take the pain. I once had a fishing hook rip clear into my thumb. Like it sliced right—"

"OK!" McKenzie said. "We get the picture."

"I don't mean pain," Mason said. "I'm talking about injuries. People get injured in football. If I break a leg in a football game, that would kill my whole wrestling season."

"I didn't mean it like I was making fun of you," Hunter explained.

"It's cool," Mason said. "What about you? Football?" Hunter didn't answer. "Hunter, you gonna play football?"

"No," Hunter finally said.

"What?" Yumi said, shocked.

Annette was surprised too. This must have been the first time Hunter had said this out loud.

"This is the second time I've been out here in serious danger in the mountains. I mean, we could . . . well, it's bad. And the thing is, being in trouble like this forces you to think about what is really important. And football is *not* important to me. I don't like it. I've been pretending to like it because that's what everybody expects. But if I get through this, I'm done pretending."

Yumi squeezed Hunter's shoulder. The group walked on, no one saying anything for a while.

"No, you know what?" Mason said. "That's cool, man. Respect. And know what else? I kind of like football. Forget what my cousin says, or if my dad thinks I have to dig in full-blast going for a state wrestling championship. You're right, Higgins. We could die out here."

"Geez, Mason," Yumi said.

"Or we could die in a car crash someday or, like . . . choking on a chicken bone or something. Maybe I won't be around to make the state wrestling tournament even if I could qualify. Might as well have a good time. You know?"

"That's cool, Mason," Morgan said.

"I'm excited for volleyball," McKenzie said. Normally McKenzie diving in to talk about herself would have been annoying, but Annette was glad for the distraction. McKenzie continued, "My mom played volleyball all through high school. Sometimes, when it's the two of us . . . it's just fun."

"I'll be right there with you," Morgan said. "I'm not very good, but . . . Well, we have to get out of this mess first."

"We will," Swann said. "If Kelton, Hunter, and I made it through that blizzard up on Storm Mountain, then this? This is like no problem."

"Swann, come on," Kelton said. He pointed to the smoke.

"No, I mean it," Swann said. "We don't have the snow to trudge through. We're not going to freeze to death just walking around. Sure, this is bad, but I know we're going to make it. And, you know what? Volleyball sounds like fun. We played it in gym this last year. I think I'll give it a try."

McKenzie sighed. "It's kind of hard to pick up just from PE. Some of us are kind of serious about it."

Annette ran a hand down over her sweaty face. *Here comes another fight.*

"Maybe it's like Mason said," Swann explained. "Maybe it's about the fun. Oh, relax, McKenzie. You can still be the big star on the team. I'd just like to try it. For fun. It is a game, isn't it?"

"Um, it's like a sport, Swann," McKenzie answered.

"So is fishing, and that's been fun," Swann said.

McKenzie made a noise that was a cross between a grunt and a groan. Annette could practically hear the girl rolling her eyes at Swann. The late August sun still blazed hot, baking Annette, the rest of the group, and the earth, but a sort of chill had settled among them.

Annette scrambled for another topic. Anything to prevent the group's mood from poisoning further. "What about . . . the skating party? Isn't there a middle school roller-skating party coming up?"

"Yeah." McKenzie's condescending tone was back. "In, like, October. Practically November."

Morgan joined her. "It's a Halloween thing and like forever away, Annette."

"Plus, roller-skating?" McKenzie said. "Baby much?"

"Hold up a second," Yumi interrupted. She talked quietly with Hunter, reviewing the map and checking her bearings on the compass. "The thing about this map. Yeah, it's a good map that shows elevation. But what it doesn't show are all the trees. I'm trying to find this more gentle slope, kind of a crack leading up the mountain, but once you're out here, it's all trees."

"For real!" Kelton said. "Same trouble I had figuring out my shortcut in the snowmobile race." He held up a hand to stop the several people who looked like they were about to protest against him calling that debacle a shortcut. "I know. I know, it didn't work out, but I'm just saying, in terms of following a route. It's hard enough to plan it on a map, and even more difficult to figure it out on the ground."

Hunter used his weed-whacker walking stick to point at a huge rock outcropping ahead and to the right of their direction of travel. "If that's a cliff right there . . ." He pointed to a spot on the map. "Maybe this cliff?" He pointed more to the south. "And it looks like it's super-steep there. See how the trees ahead, the tops of them, some are higher than others?"

Yumi tapped the map. "You're thinking that's this rise?"

"Does it matter?" McKenzie asked. "As long as we can get up the mountain and keep moving west?"

"It'll matter if we keep going up this way and run into a straight vertical cliff face, have to turn around and go back," Yumi said.

Mason stood with his hands on his hips, looking up at the mountains. "In a way you're both right. But at some point we just have to go for it, you know? Staying put is the worst we could do." He smiled at Yumi. "And I trust your estimate more than most. You have to believe in yourself."

"That's easier to do when people's lives don't depend on my decision," she said quietly.

"You got this," Annette told her.

Yumi took a deep breath. "OK, listen up! From here forward, we're going to start our ascent. It will be a little steep in some places. If I'm figuring this right, it will still be manageable. You know, pay attention to hand- and footholds. We don't want anyone slipping and falling back down the mountain."

"We've got that rope," Hunter said. "We could all tie up."

"You mean, have everybody get really close to each other the whole way up the mountain?" McKenzie asked sharply.

"Maybe save that idea until we *really* need it, Higgins," Yumi said. The terrain rose quickly, and within minutes Annette's legs burned. All around her the group puffed and grunted as they stepped up, up, up.

"Wow," Swann said. "My mom . . . bought a . . . stair-stepper . . . machine. I thought . . . it was tough."

"I'll smash that . . . stupid machine," McKenzie panted.

"I'll help you," Swann said.

The only good thing about the climb so far was that, closer to the mountain, they'd come under the shade of the pines again. This felt amazingly cooler, and had the effect of reducing some of the undergrowth. They walked on rocks and pine needles now, without having to fight too many weeds and shrubs.

"Beautiful, though," Kelton said.

"We've already climbed way higher," Mason said.

"It'll be an awesome view from the top. For real," Kelton said.

Each of them forced one step, then another, always uphill. Annette only had to grab hold of a rock higher on the slope to pull herself up a couple of times. The hill wasn't too steep. But it was constant. Up, up, up, forever.

Finally, they reached a rock shelf before they'd have to cut to the right and head up a switchback path. Trees and rocks and boulders all around.

Swann sighed. "I don't want to be a baby, but—"

"Yes, can we rest for a little bit?" Kelton leaned over, his hands on his knees. "We must have come up at least five hundred feet. Look down there."

Yumi sat on a rock. "If we're on the right path, we won't make the top of the ridge until we're up another thousand, maybe thousand five hundred feet."

"Oh no," Morgan said. "From up here you can totally see the north fire. It is getting closer."

Mason pointed south. "If this section of the mountain wasn't in the way, I bet we could see the flames to the south."

"Can anyone spare some water?" McKenzie spoke in

something like a whimper. She wasn't putting on her act-like-a-baby routine. The girl was desperate.

Yumi reached behind her back and pushed her backpack up and down. "I don't have much left, but you can have some of mine." She shook her CamelBak drinking tube. "You have a bottle or something? I can squeeze the mouthpiece and water ought to drip out." McKenzie looked like she thought that would be really hard, as she approached. Yumi wiped the mouthpiece on her sleeve. "Or I could just wipe it off, if you're willing to take the risk."

"I don't know, Yumi," said McKenzie, taking hold of the drinking tube. "Sharing someone's drinking thing might kill me." She kind of laughed, but then eagerly gulped water.

"Anyone else need a drink?" Hunter asked. "I have water left. When we reach the next stream that looks reasonably clean, I'll use my water filter pump and fill all our bottles and stuff."

Not for the first time, Annette felt terrible for leading them into this mess. "I'm sorry, everybody. I didn't figure we'd be out here so long."

McKenzie gasped the way people do when they've been so thirsty that they drink and drink as long as they can without breathing. "I swear, Annette. If you apologize about this one more time, I will throw you off the mountain."

"Right," Yumi said. "Nobody saw this coming. And even if we should have thought about the fire risk, we all still could have brought more water, other gear."

After everyone had been able to drink some water, the group continued, without anyone suggesting it out loud, to make their march up the mountain. In some areas, the way ahead grew so steep that they finally did take out the rope. Yumi tied it around her waist. Hunter and Kelton tied up next. Everyone else used it as a sort of extra handle, to help pull themselves up the steeper parts.

Except to warn about a loose stone or to point out a better way of ascending to the top of the next boulder, nobody spoke. It was as if nobody dared waste so much as a particle of energy on a single extra word.

Annette coughed. She'd been breathing heavily as she climbed, and the woods all around them had filled with more and more smoke. Her throat hurt. This was only the first ridge. Yumi had said there would be a valley after this and another rise before they could follow Hazard Creek down to Highway 95 and, she hoped, to safety. Another rise? How could she possibly make another climb like this?

Gradually, Annette faded, ceased to exist. She didn't think about her friends, her family, or even the danger they all now faced. She forgot those subjects to which her mind often wandered. She didn't care about the school newspaper or website. Gone was the surprise about Hunter's choice not to play football, about Swann declaring she'd try volleyball. Hundreds of feet lower, Annette had considered whether or not she wanted to give sports a try, but even that had faded now. All that remained was her current step. Then another. And up. Up some more. Finally the shade vanished and hot bright sunlight blasted in her face. For a brief dizzy moment her heart felt like it skipped and she worried the forest fire was in front of them. But just as quickly, some of her sense returned and she realized it was only the sun.

Annette squinted against the glare and kept walking, until finally a shadow crossed before her and put her arms around her. "Whoa, there, Ann," Yumi said. "Let's take a break. I think we've earned it."

"What are you talking about?" Annette whispered.

"We made it! To the top of the first ridge anyway." Yumi patted her back. "Woo! That was quite a thing."

Morgan practically fell down on a rock, taking a seat to rest. McKenzie stayed on her feet. Was she trying to be tough? Annette didn't know or care. She sat on a wide low flat slab of rock, pulled off her shoes and socks, and winced when she saw her feet. Angry red hotspots on the backs of her heels. The same on the toes next to her big toes. Her feet would be in bad shape before this was over.

Annette wiped her sweaty brow, took a deep breath, and finally looked around. "Wow," she whispered. If she wasn't stretched out on the warm rock, she would have almost thought she was flying. They were up on top of the world. In the distance below all around were trees, mountains, valleys. "Idaho, I love you."

Idaho was known as the gem state due to all the mining that settlers had done back in Wild West cowboy times. But the truth was the entire state was one beautiful gem of a nature place. *Except right now, the gem's on fire.*

"Hey, guys?" Hunter called out. "I know we'd all like a break, but the fire doesn't get tired. It's still spreading. We better not rest very long."

Annette sighed again, wincing as she slipped her socks and then her shoes back on. Every part of her body protested with soreness as she forced herself to her feet. Everybody drank more water. From the looks of the others, Annette knew she was not alone in her misery at being forced to continue so soon. Yumi and Hunter checked the map and her compass. And then the group set off again, the only mercy being the start of a downhill route. A small mercy, with the deadly fires burning closer and closer.

ELIZABETH WILLARD PULLED HER CAR INTO THE GARAGE AT home, shut off the engine, and closed her eyes to soak in the silence. It had been an exhausting day. The phone in her office at City Hall had not stopped ringing. The fire. The stupid fire. It was terrible, yes. But did people not have Google? The fire department and Forest Service phone numbers were right there on the McCall website. They didn't have to call the town secretary with every question, did they?

What percentage containment do they got on the fire? Check the news! They were trying to keep the line open to help organize emergency response.

Um, there's a lot of smoke. Will the city pool still be open today? Call! The! Pool!

I live in an apartment on Roosevelt Avenue. Is there an evacuation order? Do I need to leave? Hmm. She'd really had to think about that brain-buster. A block and a half from the lake. No, probably safe from having to evacuate. You could always just look out your window, and when the entire town panics and runs away, go with them.

Of course, she hadn't been able to say any of these things to the callers, and she forced herself to remember they were all good people who were simply scared. And a solid portion of the calls had been legitimate business. The mayor checking in to see if there was any word yet about National Guard firefighting reinforcements. Guardsmen were on standby at Boise. KTVB 7 News calling to talk to the mayor about some approval or other, and asking about flight clearance for their news chopper. CBS News, the national bureau, calling about sending reporters and what kind of access they could expect from city government and emergency responders and was this fire as serious as they were hearing?

Liz stepped out of the car into her garage. The fire was very serious. It was on pace to set a terrible new record, perhaps the largest fire the state had ever suffered. She shouldn't have even come home, wouldn't have come home if she didn't need to take care of the kids. Poor Annette. Poor responsible mature Annette. No, it definitely wouldn't be fair to leave her in charge of helping the younger ones even longer. Janelle had to work tonight and Kyle was busy with football pre-season practice.

She went into the house, emerging into her kitchen. She sighed. This used to be her kitchen. "Oh come on, Annette." The sink was full of dirty dishes. The dishwasher door was open, with the clean dishes from last night still in it. Someone must have needed a glass or silverware and pulled it from the dishwasher, apparently unable to summon the ambition to empty the rest of the machine. Maybe the culprit had pulled from the dishwasher the knife that was now on the counter, covered in a glob of peanut butter next to no fewer than four cheese-stick wrappers and a half-eaten sandwich.

"That's it," she muttered quietly. "You kids are going to face some serious punishment." She called out. "I'm home!" No answer. She yelled louder. "Hello?"

"Hey, Mom," Gabe called from the living room.

She stepped over one of Dakota's Lego creations in the dining room and went to see Gabe. There he was in front of the TV, playing video games. "Have you been playing games all day?" He didn't answer. "Gabe!"

The kid jumped a little. "What?"

"Have you been playing that thing all day?"

"No," Gabe said. "I had to pause it once in a while to go to the bathroom."

"Where's Dakota? Where's Annette?" Again no answer. She grabbed the remote control and shut the TV off.

"Mom! No! The game is still going! You can't just shut off the TV!"

Liz glared at her son. "Don't even try to turn that TV back on, or I swear, I'll throw that X-Whatever-It's-Called straight in the trash. Where's Dakota?"

Gabe stretched and rubbed his eyes. "I don't know. Upstairs playing Legos, I think."

Throwing the video games away would probably be the best thing for him. "Where's Annie?"

"She left," Gabe said.

What was this kid talking about? Annette left? That was unlikely.

"Said she was meeting some friends to go fishing." Gabe shrugged. "I don't know. She left us sandwiches, though. They weren't very good. Mine had too much—"

"When did she leave? Went fishing where?"

Gabe yawned. "She left this morning right after you did. Dakota was outside awhile, said the Gator is gone." He held his hands up. "I said she'd be in a lot of trouble, but—"

"Where did she go!"

Gabe seemed to concentrate hard about that one for a long moment. "What was it? Some pond."

That didn't help at all. There were a zillion ponds all around McCall. "Think, Gabe! This is important! Where did she say she was going?"

"A pond!" Gabe burst out. "I don't know. I was playing my game. Wasn't really listening." Then he perked up. "Oh. She said something about paint maybe?"

Liz dropped her purse right in the middle of the living room floor and pressed her hands to her chest. *Oh no. Oh Lord God Almighty. Please no. Please let the kid be wrong.* "Gabe, now think. Did she say Painted Pond?"

"Yeah!" Gabe smiled brightly. He always had such a cute smile. "That's it." He must have noticed her terror. "Why? What's the big deal? Dad and her been fishing there a bunch of times."

Tears welled in Liz's eyes, and she grabbed the back of the sofa as dizziness swept through her. *Oh no. My sweet baby. No.* Elizabeth Willard had been looking at fire updates on the big wall map in City Hall all day. She knew where Painted Pond was. Way up north, on the other side of what was quickly becoming the worst wildfire in her lifetime. "Get your brother. Bring him down here. Start picking this place up. No more games."

"But *Mom*," Gabe whined.

"Just do it! Right now!" She felt terrible for yelling at her son, even as she did it, but she'd have to worry about that later. Her daughter was in deadly danger. "That's if she's still—" She wouldn't allow herself to finish the sentence. The thought was unspeakable. "I have to make some calls."

CHAPTER 10

"COME ON!" YUMI CALLED TO THE OTHERS. "WE HAVE TO go faster!" They were scrambling down the other side of the ridge. Some parts of the downslope were very steep, and she'd led the way, sliding down the rock. Mason had talked about how fire, with its heat rising, naturally went uphill very quickly. They had to climb down into the thick woods and abundant fire fuel supply at the base of the valley ahead of them, and then climb all the way up over the top of the next ridge.

She reached a small cliff, a drop of six to eight feet. Quickly, Yumi pocketed her compass, scooted to the edge, and jumped, rolling out on the pine needles below, a rock jabbing into her side as she did so. "It's not that high. You have to jump. If I can do it, you can." She wanted to throw up, because she was hungry and terrified, and because the way she sounded reminded her of one of those horrible win-at-all-costs sports coaches she saw in the movies.

Hunter was right behind her. He rubbed his leg, which had been broken and in a cast all winter.

"You can do it, Higgins," Yumi said. "Trust me."

It was the *trust me* that seemed to act like a trigger, a switch. Hunter eased himself to the edge and jumped. Kelton, having watched the other two, quickly followed. Then Annette jumped. The others gathered at the top.

Swann hesitated, perched at the edge. "No princess," she said quietly as she jumped.

McKenzie shook her head. "No way." She flipped over on her belly, lowering her legs. Mason directed her to footholds. She climbed down, losing it about halfway, and she was forced to awkwardly jump.

Morgan froze in fear. She looked around for a different way down, but the little cliff ran a long way to either side.

"We don't have time to wait!" Yumi shouted. "Hurry up!"

Annette put her hand on her arm and whispered. "It's OK, Yumi. I get the frustration, but we don't want to freak her out even more."

Mason, still up there with Morgan, whispered to her. She nodded. "I'm going to help lower her down. You guys kind of grab on to her to help her the rest of the way."

Yumi bit her lip. Annette was right, and her touch had helped calm her a little. But this wasn't much of a drop. It was like jumping off equipment back on the elementary school playground.

"Come on, Morgan," McKenzie said. "This is kind of pathetic. I mean, can you, like, put on a bigger drama show?"

"I'm scared," Morgan whimpered.

Yumi was scared too. They were all frightened, even McKenzie. And that was what made McKenzie so mean. *Do you want to be like McKenzie?* Yumi asked herself. *Yelling at her own best friend and making the situation worse?* No. She did not. "That-a-way, Morgan. You can do it."

Mason put his wrestling muscles to good use, holding Morgan's hands and lowering her to the others. Kelton, Hunter, and Swann took easy hold of her and lowered her to the ground. Mason crouched, placed one hand on the rock, and side-vaulted, landing gracefully, bending his legs. He smiled.

Higgins slapped the guy a high five. Kelton patted his shoulder. OK, maybe Mason had made a mistake in letting himself be suckered into this fishing trip with McKenzie and Morgan, but she had to admit Mason was a cool guy.

Annette squeezed Morgan in a one-arm side hug. "Don't worry. You're cool. You're good. We're right with you."

"Where do we go from here?" Swann asked.

Yumi hated that question. She took a deep breath, looking up at the smoke rising on the side of the mountain from which they'd come. Hunter held up the map and she checked her compass. She tried to do her best to remember everything her dad had taught her about land navigation. But learning how to understand and use a map and compass was different from figuring out where to go on the ground. The map didn't take trees, rocks, or other obstacles like that little cliff into account.

And there was one other problem. A possibility so horrible

she didn't want to admit it even to herself, the thought that twisted around inside her and made her want to drop to the ground and curl up in a ball. They all asked her which way to go, but she wasn't completely sure. She didn't know with absolute certainty. She was doing her best, but she was still partly guessing. Stumped on a quiz at school? A guess was a good idea. She might get lucky, and if she didn't, no big deal. But if she was wrong now, with the fire closing in, they were all dead.

That was part of the reason she'd been yelling at everybody to hurry. If they moved faster, they might earn enough time to reroute, to go back and choose a different path, to correct for a bad choice. So she understood why McKenzie was acting extra-mean. But there had to be a way for Yumi to handle this without acting like her.

Maybe she could play the part of the cheerleader. "Follow me," she said as she trotted off in what she thought was the right direction. "This valley isn't very deep, so not as much of a climb up to the next ridge. But we need to hurry to get there."

The only thing almost as strange and uncomfortable as trying to lead the way through the wilderness was the fact that everybody listened to her. When she picked the route, the others followed. When she told them to hurry, she could tell that they tried. Since her mother was Japanese, Yumi had always felt a little "other" in the almost exclusively white town of McCall. Once or twice one idiot or another had asked her where she was from.

"McCall," she'd say.

"No, but what country?" they'd say.

It was like that. As little kids, nobody had ever said she couldn't play with them because she was half Japanese. She wasn't ever in the outcast situation that, until recently, Kelton Fielding had endured, but she'd remained a little bit of an outsider. People like McKenzie or Swann had ideas that everyone else embraced. Now they were following her. Yumi had often thought she would have enjoyed being the one to whom everyone else listened, but now that the responsibility was hers, she hated it.

As they finally reached the dense woods at the base of the valley, Annette caught up with her. "That smoke is really thick at the top of the mountain behind us." She leaned closer and spoke more quietly. "Yumi, are we going to make it? Is there another way? A faster way?"

"I'm doing the best I can!" Yumi hissed. "You're the straight-A genius student. If you think you can do better, you lead the way!" Annette seemed to shrink or wilt as soon as Yumi had lashed out at her. Yumi squeezed her itchy smoky eyes closed for a moment. *You're an idiot, Yumi.* "I'm sorry," she said.

"No, I'm sorry," Annette said. "I really messed things up between us, first when I wrote that stupid school paper article, and then getting us into this mess."

Yumi put her hand on Annette's shoulder. "Listen. I'm the one who should apologize. I shouldn't have snapped at you. And the thing about that article. It's just that the whole war was, in some way, about people kissing up to either of two super-popular girls. It drove me crazy when it looked like you were kissing up the same way. I thought, let them tear each other apart. What's it to us?"

"Makes sense, in a way, I guess," Annette said after a moment.

"Well, no, it doesn't," Yumi said. "Swann's pretty cool. And if we escape this fire situation and I get the chance to get to know McKenzie, I'd probably see she's OK too."

"We'll escape," Annette said with confidence. "I didn't mean to suggest you don't know the way."

"But I don't," Yumi admitted quietly to Annette so the others wouldn't hear. "I think I'm right, but I'm basically just making my best guess. If I'm wrong—"

"You're not wrong," Annette said. "You're Yumi Higgins, and . . . and you're my best friend, and you can do anything."

Yumi didn't know what to say to that. She was never very good at talking all mushy about feelings. She only smiled and nodded as they continued crunching through the thick dry undergrowth. Then she checked her compass and pointed in the direction she thought they should go. "This is it," Yumi called out to everyone. The mountain wasn't one even, steep slope all the way up. There was a kind of shelf, like a massive ramp, that ran diagonally up the side. Again, she could identify the major land feature on the map, but locating it in the woods wasn't easy. "I'm pretty sure this is the easiest route." But could they make the next rise before the flames caught up with them?

"You're pretty sure?" McKenzie asked. Yumi shot her a

helpless look. McKenzie held her hands up in surrender. "Or maybe there's no time to make absolutely sure. I get you."

"Right now," Yumi explained, "all we know is we can't stay here. We have to push one more hard climb, and then . . . and then I think we can follow the course of the stream all the way. Downhill clear to the highway."

Mason leaned back against the trunk of a large pine. "Do any of you also feel like you're about to pass out? I know we have to do this, but I don't know how I can."

"We'll have to stop for water and to eat sometime," Morgan said. "We aren't machines. We're going to need to rest and refuel."

"Right, then," Annette said. "Let's hurry up this next climb as fast as we can. If we're tough, and if we're lucky, we'll earn a little rest time at the top."

Yumi's legs burned as she pushed off, heaving up the slope. Although the terrain was slightly easier, the climb was not. It didn't matter how tough someone was. At a certain point, everyone reached their limit. They were nearly out of energy. Whether that was solely the result of being on the run and climbing for hours, or the physical work combined with the terror of the coming fire, Yumi didn't know. But she was certain the fire was only gaining strength as it moved. She and the rest of them were not.

Filtered through the thick smoke, the sun shined blood-red in the afternoon sky, so heavily filtered they could easily look at it with no pain save for the itchiness of the surrounding smoke in their eyes.

People talked about climbing and reaching the tops of mountains as if it were like climbing up onto the top of a house, where at first you struggle, but then you're sitting on the shingles, clearly on the roof. A mountain wasn't like that. There was no line to mark that point at which one was no longer climbing, but had reached the top. There was no single location at which one began to descend down the other side. There were lots of smaller rises and gullies on the massive rounded top of the ridge.

After a long time, and without the energy to talk about it much, they began to realize they weren't fighting uphill as much anymore.

"It's getting dark," Morgan said. "But it's hours until sunset. From the smoke? How dark is it going to get?"

Nobody answered her. And nobody said anything as, one by one, they took seats on rocks or fallen logs in the diminishing light. Swann and Kelton produced the big cans of pudding and beans. Kelton started opening them. Hunter offered two sleeves of crackers. The group gathered around their stolen meal.

"Chocolate pudding, cold baked beans, and crackers," McKenzie said. "I'm hungry enough to eat anything." They dug in with spoons Swann had taken from the cabin, slowly at first, then faster, like hungry animals. McKenzie laughed after a while, a smear of brown pudding and cracker crumbs on her cheek. "This is so sick."

Hunter stood up after a while. "I noticed a little stream on the way up. I'll go fill our CamelBaks."

"You sure that water's safe to drink?" Morgan asked.

Hunter smiled. "I have a filter pump. It'll be fine." He pointed at everyone gathered around the cans. "Anyway, it can't be much more gross than this."

"Nobody goes alone, Higgins," Yumi said. If he got lost or hurt, he'd be in big trouble on his own.

"I'll go," Annette said quickly.

What was that about? Yumi met her friend's eyes as if to ask if she was sure. Annette nodded and was on her feet with Hunter, heading in the direction from which they'd come.

"I can handle this on my own, you know," Hunter said after they'd reached the water source. Perhaps in early spring the stream might be impressive, but this late in a mostly rainless summer, it was reduced to a low trickle, sprinkling in a little waterfall down the mossy rock. Hunter produced his small handheld pump, one plastic tube in the stream, and the other in his open CamelBak water bladder. It would take many squeezes, but he'd have the thing filled soon enough.

"Sure," Annette said, scuffing her shoe in the dirt on the secluded rock ledge where they stood. "But it's like Yumi said."

Hunter smiled, getting soaked in the stream, still pumping. "So you're here to protect me?"

"Something like that," Annette said. Why had she offered to go with him? It would have been so much easier to simply lie there and rest on that flat stone area she'd found. She'd volunteered without thinking. Or had she, on the instinctual level to which they'd all been reduced in this ordeal, simply understood she needed to work things out with Hunter the way she'd fixed things with Yumi? *Well, but maybe not in the exact same way.*

And suddenly Annette, who worked with words so much, found she had no idea what to say. At first it worried her, embarrassed her, but against the dangerous situation they faced, her silence didn't seem so awkward. And Hunter smiled kindly.

"I think I wore the totally wrong dress to the dance last night," she blurted out.

Hunter tilted his head, confused, she guessed, and wondering why she would bring that up now. "But you looked, you know . . . I mean, it was—"

"I wore it because I wanted to impress you," Annette said. And, tired as she was, it was a tremendous relief to admit that. "It was the fanciest dress I could find, and I thought if I wore it, I might look even a little bit pretty and—"

"Annette, you're so beautiful."

She stepped toward him in a rush, right under the cool rain of the little stream, and her hand touched his soft cheek and her lips pressed to his. She felt his surprised intake of breath. He took a half step back, before seeming to decide what to do. Their lips parted and they embraced, watching each other in this deep serious way she'd never known before. Then they kissed again, softer and warmer and longer this time. Annette had no idea what she was doing, but somehow she understood that was OK because Hunter didn't either.

They parted again, breathing heavy. Her heart pounded, from something besides fear and exertion for the first time that day, from something wonderful. She'd come to the woods because she'd wanted to make a story of her own. Somehow she knew, even then, that this story she shared with Hunter would be one she remembered for a very long time.

After a moment, she became aware of glittering sparkles on the falling water around them.

She followed Hunter's gaze across the valley to the first mountain ridge they'd crossed. There the fire devoured everything it touched and spread to burn more.

Annette touched her forehead to Hunter's and whispered. "I read somewhere that you never forget your first kiss." She nodded toward the inferno. "No chance I'll ever forget this."

"I've wanted to do that since this last fall when you came hunting with us," Hunter said quietly.

"Me too," Annette said. She could hardly believe it had really happened. She could still feel an echo of the pressure of his lips on hers. "But the fire," she said. "We should probably—"

A loud angry curse sounded from above them. Yumi. "Higgins! Annette! Where are you! Fire's coming! We gotta go!"

"What took you so long?" Swann demanded when Hunter and Annette finally returned to the rest of the group. "And you just filled up the one CamelBak?"

Yumi watched the two of them, soaking wet and smiling. Neither of them would meet her eyes. Yumi smiled as well.

Something had happened while the two of them were away. Something big. But there was no time to talk about it now. Instead she pulled them both close and spoke quietly. "The three of us *will* talk later. If we don't die." To everyone else she shouted, "Fire's coming. Rest time is over. If you need water, ask Hunter. Let's move."

Kelton groaned as he rose to his feet. "Move where?"

Yumi glanced at the fire closing in from the east, felt the wind shifting, gaining intensity, and for a moment she wasn't sure exactly which way to go. The smoke had reduced visibility so that navigating by general compass direction and landmarks was becoming impossible. But then she saw it. She pointed toward the blood-red sun. "It's the only thing this smoke is good for. It cuts out the view of just about everything else except . . . see? The dark outlines? Shadows of the mountain. Hard to see, but notice that dark V right there?" She pointed to the map. "What do you want to bet *that* is our creek valley?"

"I guess I'll bet my life," Hunter said.

"You bet your . . . yeah, I guess you'll bet your life," Yumi said. "I think we're just about right where we're supposed to be! Still on course!" She reached out to squeeze Annette's hand but found it already holding Hunter's hand.

"Oh," Yumi said. They were in mortal danger, but she was still stunned to realize what she'd always thought would happen between Higgins and Annette had finally happened. "Right."

"Let's go!" McKenzie shouted.

Yumi led the way, and the group moved out. It was easy at

first, but after about a minute, Kelton shouted, "Fire! There's fire down there, too!"

In the near distance to the southwest, down in the hazy valley, were three . . . no, four . . . unmistakable white orange blobs of fire. Anyone moving slowly or half-asleep at that point jumped quickly to alertness.

"How's that possible?" Morgan cried. "It's not like we've been sitting up here forever taking a nap."

"The fire was far away!" McKenzie protested. "It obviously hasn't burned over us yet. How could there be fire down there?"

The group was descending into panic. Mason waved his hands over his head. "Hey. *Hey!*"

"Shut up!" Annette screamed. Yumi looked at her in surprise. Annette was not the sort of person she'd ever expect to try to shout everyone down, the last person she'd expect to succeed at it. "How the fire got down there doesn't really matter now. Freaking out won't help us. Let's move."

Yumi pointed toward the valley. "That fire down there is still to the south of where we have to go. It's a race, is all. We have to win."

CHAPTER 11

THE STRANGEST MIX OF EMOTIONS SWIRLED WITHIN Annette. She shook with terror from the fire closing in on them, and yet at the same time she could not stop smiling about what had happened with Hunter. If not for the world burning up all around them, it would have been the perfect fairy-tale storybook kiss. They all hurried after Yumi like they were characters in some apocalypse movie. She laughed to herself. She'd never imagined she'd be so happy in the apocalypse.

Yumi glanced her way, dirt streaked on her forehead and cheek, sweat rolling down her face. She half smiled and rolled her eyes. "You have to stop. I've been telling you and Higgins to make a move for almost a year, and you pick now? We're all going to die, and you two choose *now* to get together?"

Annette giggled. "I know! I'm sorry. It just kind of happened. Taking advantage of our last chance, I guess."

"It won't be your last chance, as long as we can find our way down off this mountain," Yumi said.

"You know," Annette said quietly to Yumi, "this is horrible.

I'd rather we were safe at your house playing *Call of Duty* or that zombie game. But you're kind of an action hero in all this. Way cooler than anyone on those games."

Yumi shrugged away the idea. "The characters I play on my games don't get tired. Their maps are better. And usually in the game there's a limited area of operations."

"Well." Annette patted her back. It was gritty and soaked with sweat. "I'd still rather be with you."

"Then you're an idiot," Yumi said. But she smiled, and slapped Annette on the shoulder. Yumi was direct and her sense of humor put some people off, but Annette was glad to count her as a friend.

Yumi cursed loud enough to be heard all the way back in McCall.

"What's the matter?" Hunter raced ahead to catch up with her. "Are you hurt?"

Yumi held her arms out to the side, as if she were trying to form a barrier as she stepped backward, cursing again. A few paces ahead, she remained turned away from everyone, shaking, with her hands pressed to her face.

"More fire?" Swann moved closer, and put her hands on Yumi's shoulders. Yumi shook her head, and Swann saw it. They all did. About twenty yards ahead, a wide chasm, an enormous crack in the mountain.

As they approached, they quickly saw it was way too steep and deep to climb down and back up the other side. It was about six feet across—they couldn't jump over it. Smoke everywhere. White bits of ash falling like snow.

"It's OK." Swann squeezed Yumi's shoulders. "We'll be OK. We'll find another way."

Yumi shook off Swann's hold and spun to face her. "How? Fly? We don't have time for this! And with all this smoke, who knows how long this stupid crack goes? It's not on the map!"

It was not only Morgan crying now. This ravine, with the fire closing in, put the dead back in dead-end.

"Oh come on, man!" Kelton shouted. "We are so screwed. For real!"

"There has to be another way," McKenzie said. "Are you reading that map right?"

"You want the map, McKenzie?" Yumi shouted. "Take it! You lead the way. See if you can do better."

"We don't have time to do better!" McKenzie yelled.

The idea hit Annette hard and fast. "Hatchet!"

"My favorite book?" Hunter asked.

"Annette, this is not the time for a book talk," McKenzie said.

Annette dropped her backpack, and felt around inside for the hatchet she'd taken from the cabin. She slipped off its leather cover and pointed the hatchet at a thick, tall dead tree standing about twenty feet from the ravine. "That's our bridge!" Annette ran for the tree. She aimed near the bottom of the trunk and slammed the hatchet blade hard, chipping wood. "If we hurry."

"What?" Morgan asked incredulously. "You're a lumberjack now? It will take forever to cut that big thing down with that tiny ax."

Annette kept chopping, as hard and fast as she could. "The wood is dead. It'll come apart fast." She hoped she was right.

Hunter stepped beside her. "Give it here. Let me have a crack at it."

"I can do it," Annette said. She had to do it. She got her friends into this deadly situation. She had to try to get them out. She swung that hatchet again and again, and the thud of the blade on wood shook through her arm. Sweat poured down her body. The world was descending into darkness as thicker smoke rolled in around them. Her shoulder ached. Her bicep burned. A flying wood chip stung her cheek. She grunted and chopped.

"Annette, you're going to wear yourself out. Give a fresh arm a chance," Mason said. "None of us here is tough enough to chop this thing down by ourselves."

Finally she stopped and, without looking, held out the hatchet. Hunter grabbed it and with a primitive growl attacked the trunk.

"Let's push it from the other side!" Kelton said. "Careful to stay out of the way of the chopping, but let's push the tree from the other side, and we'll knock it down faster!"

Kelton and Mason slammed their shoulders into the tree. McKenzie and Swann reached above them, hands pushing on the rough wood. Eventually they all got into a rocking movement, a series of shoves to try to get the trunk shaking back and forth.

Hunter chopped and chopped. He did look tough. But the fire grew closer. It had to be coming up their ridge by now.

Hunter handed off to Mason. He hit the tree like a maniac, winding up and twisting his whole body into hard, deep chops. After a while Kelton took a turn.

"Come on!" McKenzie cried.

"It's not working!" Morgan said.

The tree cracked. Kelton chopped. The others pushed, and there was a loud deep crunch. The big dead trunk leaned. Kelton smiled and chopped more. "Come on! Push!"

More cracking.

"Kel, get out of the way!" Annette shouted. She reached out to push him clear, but stopped herself for fear that he'd hit her or himself with the hatchet.

With a loud series of cracks, the big trunk fell over and smashed to the ground, the top of it protruding out over the ravine.

"It's not long enough to reach across," Morgan said.

McKenzie pushed her filthy hair away from her face and put her hands on the tree. "Then we push it! We only have to slide it a few feet."

"It must weigh hundreds of pounds." Morgan leaned down to the tree.

The rest of them took positions around the trunk. Annette gripped a nub where a branch had long ago broken off, her blistered hands burning.

"OK," Kelton said. "On three and then *go*, got it?"

They counted off and then with grunts and groans the whole group pushed hard. At first nothing happened. Annette adjusted her grip, dipped down lower, and dug her feet in. "Come on, everybody! We can do this! Push!"

The log moved. An inch. Two inches. Mason let loose a howl. Morgan bit her lip. Yumi pumped her legs. McKenzie cursed the log while she shoved. Three inches. The log was moving now.

"Keep pushing!" McKenzie screamed.

All of them, working together with all their strength, picked up a little momentum and a slight downslope until the far end of the log smashed into an upward-sloping rock on the far side.

Annette wanted to collapse, to rest her aching body after the frantic effort, but there was no time. "Let's go!"

"Is it safe?" Morgan asked.

Kelton grunted as he gave the trunk a hard shake. It wiggled a little, and some loose gravel fell into the depths.

"Safer than that fire," Annette said. She could see the orange glow rising from the east edge of the ridge. A lot of them coughed in the thick smoke, which even rolled out of this section of the crack. A peek over the edge revealed hot snakes of flame working through whatever had once grown way down there.

The group waited around for a moment, and Annette knew, somehow, they were all trying to decide who would go first. Annette was about to say something when Yumi jumped up on the log, took a deep breath, and with her arms out to her sides for balance, ran across, jumping down on the other side.

She flashed a quick smile. "Easy," she called back.

"There's nothing to grab on to," Morgan objected. "And it has to be a thousand feet down."

"Yeah, into fire," Yumi said. "But the log is wide enough to mostly run normally. Keep moving and you'll be fine."

Hunter was across before Yumi was even done talking. Swann let out an excited scream as she crossed. Then went Kelton, McKenzie, and Morgan, a little more slowly. As soon as she hesitated, Mason rushed onto the log behind her.

"Just step, step, step," he told her calmly. "You're good. I'm right behind you."

"I hate this, I hate this, I hate this," Morgan whimpered. "I am *not* a baby!" she shouted. "This is stupid-dangerous and any sane person would be scared."

"Morgie, I'm scared too. We just have to—"

"Did you just call me *Morgie?*" She stopped so suddenly that it threw her off balance. She pinwheeled her arms. "No, no. You guys!"

Annette's hands sweated as she watched. A small crack near the thicker end of the log on her side widened. A snapping sound. A low thud. The log shook, rolling a little. Morgan screamed.

"Run!" Yumi screamed, reaching out her hand from the far side.

"Annette, hurry!" Hunter shouted.

Mason hooked his arms beneath Morgan's armpits, lifted with a grunt, and ran, jumping, with Morgan, into the waiting arms of the whole panicked group.

It all happened in a couple of seconds, and yet, to Annette, time stretched, so that an instant dragged to eternity, and the old tree, scraping, cracking, and thudding down the rocky sides of the chasm to the fires below, signaled with each sound it made, the cruel certainty that Annette was trapped. She was doomed.

Everyone was quiet for a long time. From the near distance, fire crackled. From somewhere came the loud snap-crunch of what had to be a whole tree succumbing to the fire.

Morgan sobbed. "Oh no." Tears rolled down her face. "Annette, I am so sorry. I am so, so sorry. If I had hurried. If I hadn't froze up like that, you would have had time to cross. Now . . . now what are we going to do?" Sitting in the dirt, she looked around helplessly at the others. "What are we going to do?"

Annette stared at the wide-open gap before her. At least six feet. Maybe a little more. She looked at the others. Hunter. Kelton. Swann. They all stared back, sad and helpless. Even Yumi, who had seemed like an action hero half the day, stood with tears in her eyes, apparently out of options.

"Doesn't something like this happen in *Snowtastrophe III?*" Annette asked. She smiled sadly at Swann. "Like Lieutenant Whatshisname, played by Ricky Wu, is trying to get that reporter girl to safety, but the ice gives out between them, and your dad, the Lord of the Vampires, is closing in on his snowmobile. He's cut off."

"Annette," Swann said. "That's just a stupid movie. The ravine was all cushions in the bottom. Computer tricks made it look deep. And the scene was filmed with stunt doubles who were on wires for the whole jump across."

Annette smiled. "There you go, Swann. Great idea."

Swann looked at Kelton. "Did she hit her head or something? Dehydration getting to her?"

Annette explained. "This time it will be the reporter girl making the jump. No stunt doubles or cushions involved, but we will have a safety wire." She rushed to her backpack, pulled out the rope, and tied her end of the rope around her waist, weaving it through the belt loops on her jeans for good measure.

Yumi frowned, hands on her hips. "What are you . . . No, Ann, come on. This is stupid."

"Yes, it is!" Annette proclaimed. "Dumbest thing I've ever done." She spun the other end around and around above her head rodeo-style, before throwing it over to the others. Kelton caught it. He stared at the rope in wonder. "This *is* dumb, but so is waiting around over here to be burned alive. So, this is how it's going to work. There are seven of you. One of me. Enough rope to give me a bit of a running start. I'll run and jump. Morgan, you hold the rope in front. Once you see I've jumped, you yell to pull. Then everybody pull fast as you can. That way if I don't quite make it, you can help haul me up to safety."

Hunter glanced around at the others, even as he took hold of the rope. "Annette, are you sure about this?"

No, she was absolutely not sure about this. How could he ask that? Maybe Ricky Wu's character on *Snowtastrophe III* never had doubts, but she was no bodybuilder martial-arts-specialist actor like Ricky Wu. "I'm going to jump whether or not you help me, so if you want to sit back and do nothing, while I fall to a bone-crushing fiery death . . . hey, that's cool, I guess."

"Here," Mason said. "Let's wrap the rope around our waists too. We'll have to stand close together. Closer. I'm probably heaviest, so I'll be the anchor in the back."

It took a while for the others to get set up. In the end, there wasn't enough room for everyone to tie in, so Morgan and McKenzie agreed to stay off the rope and stand by the edge to help catch Annette as she came over.

Mason locked his hands on the rope. "OK. This here is like fishing. Get it? We already have the catch on the line. Once we start, there's no second-guessing, no hesitation, and definitely no stopping until we reel her in. Soon's Morgan says go, we pull, pull, pull, and don't stop pulling no matter what happens."

They all murmured agreement and Annette backed up as far as the rope would let her. She'd never make this jump, never vault over and land on her feet on the other side. This would end in a painful hard scramble up the rocks.

Tears rolled down Morgan's face. Annette wished the girl would pull herself together—her emotional display was cracking Annette's control. If she had any chance at this jump, she had to give it her all. She had to be hard-core.

"Whenever you're ready, Ann," Yumi called to her.

But this wasn't a whenever-you're-ready type of situation. The fire was coming. She could feel the waves of hot breeze already. She couldn't afford to lose time, and the more she thought about what she had to do, the more afraid she became.

In her head, this would work. She didn't weigh that much, not close to as much as the combined weight of the seven others. She was securely tied to the rope. With a good run and jump, and with their pull, she'd make it. She would. She would. Right now. She lowered into something like a runner's starter stance. Now. Her muscles twitched. Now. One of the quotes she'd copied into her notebook echoed in her mind. *The Lord of the Rings* author, J. R. R. Tolkien, once said, "Courage is found in unlikely places." She finally knew what that meant. She breathed deeply, in and out through her nose. In and out. And—her legs exploded, launching her forward, arms pumping.

Annette screamed, slapping her foot down on the rocky edge and pushing off hard.

"Pull!" Morgan called.

Darkness laced with fire below, hot sparks rising up to greet her. Hard yank to her back, like being punched in the spine.

Stone and scrub brush slammed her chest and legs, head smacking her forearm. No breath. She slipped down for a second. Her feet kicked in the endless empty air below.

"Pull!Pull!Pull!" someone shouted.

Annette hurt all over. She wanted to help them, wanted to climb, but pain pulsed through her chest, legs, arms. She couldn't breathe!

Hands gripped her arms, pulling her up.

"Got you," Morgan cried. "You're OK."

"Don't worry. Come on up," McKenzie echoed. To the

others she shouted, "We got her! Stop pulling! We're dragging her right over the rock!"

There was no answer to McKenzie's complaint, and a moment later Annette was on flat ground again. She could almost get a breath in.

Everyone surrounded her, patting her, asking if she was OK.

"Hey!" Yumi said sharply. "Let's give her some room. Let her get some air. Maybe move her farther from the edge. Annette, can you walk?"

She couldn't do anything. She opened her mouth and tried to suck in a breath.

"She hit so hard," Morgan said. "Maybe she broke a rib?"

"Wind . . ." Annette gasped. "Winded."

"Higgins, Kelton, help me," Yumi said. The boys ducked, draping her arms over their shoulders, and then the three of them hauled Annette a solid twenty feet from the chasm. "Annette, that had to have hurt bad. But is anything broken? Can you walk? If you can move, we should all go."

Annette nodded, sucking in half a breath. She took a step. Then another. The pain was diminishing. "How would I know if something's broken?"

"Oh, trust me," said Hunter, risking sliding out from under her arm. She wished he hadn't. "If something's broken, you'll know."

Annette took a few more steps. McKenzie approached and put a hand on Annette's shoulder. "That looked like it hurt bad.

And it had to have been terrifying. But, Annette, it looks like you're kind of walking. Yumi's right. We should go. I'm sorry."

Annette smiled. It was obvious McKenzie was sincere. She seemed to feel bad pushing Annette after what had just happened. But she was also right. Annette placed her hand on McKenzie's shoulder and smiled. "Yeah. I can kind of breathe now. I can walk." She winced as she looked at the horrible red skin scrapes on her arms and legs. "Everything else, I'll figure out on the way. All that matters is fleeing the fire."

FIRE CHIEF NICK PANETTI TWISTED THE CAP OFF A COLD BOTTLE of water and started chugging. He hated wildfires. He really did. He loved the thrill of battling against them and the feeling that he was doing something useful and important, saving people and their homes from the blaze. But he hated these fires. Worse than that, though, he hated the press when they showed up to report on the fires.

"Chief Panetti!" A woman called, holding out her phone to record. "Chief Panetti, any idea what caused this blaze?"

Another reporter, a man with a ridiculous large mustache straight out of 1977, raised his hand. "Chief Panetti, is the city of McCall itself in danger?"

What percentage of the fire is contained at this time? Is it true that you are now battling multiple fires? Any idea if or when the governor might declare a state of emergency or a disaster area? What is meant when people talk about a fire being contained? Is there any hope of extinguishing this blaze without the help of significant rainfall?

Panetti closed his eyes and pressed his fist against the throbbing pain in his forehead, though whether the pain came from his drinking ice-cold water too fast or from the irritation from the reporters, he could not say.

"Hey, one at a time, please," Panetti said. "One—" The reporters all talked at once. Why did they always do this? "One. . . . please. Ladies and gentlemen, if you could please—"

"Everybody quiet!" Sheriff Hamlin shouted. "Panetti has a lot of work to do. He's been kind enough to agree to answer your questions. But he's going to call on you to ask one at a time, or this conference is over."

Panetti offered his old friend Hank Hamlin a half smile. Even now that he was getting older, he was so tough. He'd been an animal back in high school when the two of them had played football together. But that was a long time ago, with no dangerous fire and no annoying reporters to deal with. Panetti pointed to the woman with the phone. "What's your question?"

The woman offered a tight smile. "Chief Panetti, more and more resources are rushing to fight this blaze, and yet all reports seem to indicate that it only continues to spread. Can you explain that, and can you estimate when this fire might finally be contained?"

The chief stared at the reporter for a moment, and decided to give her the benefit of the doubt. She was probably smarter than the question she had just asked, and was merely trying to get him to explain the answer for the benefit of the many people who were worried about this fire. "Listen, as I've said before, as you've heard from any of the men involved in fighting this fire, we haven't seen anything like this in our careers. I've been fighting wildfires for twenty-two years, and this is, by far, the worst combination of circumstances I've ever seen. We were both lucky and unlucky the last two years, with enough snow and rainfall to keep the wilderness from becoming too dry and presenting too much of a fire risk. Unfortunately, that's a good news/bad news situation. Yes, for the last two years the moisture reduced fire risk, but it also helped grow a lot of fuel. Then this spring and summer have brought far below normal rainfall, so all that fuel dried out.

Our other problem is that we're facing very high winds today. We're seeing the convergence of two air pressure systems, which is playing havoc with wind direction. This places our firefighters at greater risk. They may be set up to defend a structure or key transportation route, only to have the wind shift, altering the direction and pattern of the fire's spread. This has the potential to cut off escape routes for our firefighters. So right now a lot of our efforts are on evacuation and the safety of our own people, trying to do the best we can to contain the spread of this fire."

Chris Terine, one of his men, not the best firefighter in the field but an ace when it came to organization, communication, and administration, stepped up to the lectern and pulled him back a few steps. He was a solid guy and wouldn't interrupt something like this if it wasn't really important. Panetti held up a finger. "Excuse me, just one second, folks."

Terine handed him a note card with the worst possible news. He squeezed his eyes shut for a moment. The card read, *Missing kids. Possibly fishing in fire zone*, with the names of the potentially missing kids written in a neat column. Beneath the names was written, *Possibly in vicinity of Painted Pond.* "Right." He nodded his thanks and dismissal to his man and stepped back to the microphone. He took a deep breath. He hated dealing with the press, and he hated having to relay this news even more.

One of the press men raised a pen. "Chief Panetti, are there any plans to issue an evacuation order for—"

Panetti held up his hand. "In a minute. Listen up. I've just received information I want to pass along to you, and I'll preface everything I'm about to say by reminding everybody to remain calm." There was a concerned murmur among the press. A couple of locals who had been volunteering to get food and water to firefighters on break at this command post stepped into the tent.

"First of all, I must demand that every parent in the McCall area immediately verify the location of their children. In fact, it would be best if the kids just went home and stayed there. Even if you think you know where your kids are, I'm telling you to contact them and make sure you know. I say that because our situation is complicated by . . ." He counted the names on the list. "Eight missing children. At this time, the sheriff's office and the fire department are interested in any information about the location of the following young people. Annette Willard. Swann Siddiq. Hunter Higgins. Yumi Higgins. Kelton Fielding. McKenzie Crenner. Morgan Vaughn. Mason Bridger." The reporters rushed to ask questions but Panetti held up a hand and spoke loudly. "We have some reason to believe that they may have been in the area or . . ." Panetti surveyed the map of his memory. Where was Painted Pond? Up north of where the first fire started, for sure. "North of the area where this fire started."

"Do you mean there are children trapped in the fire?" some reporter called from the back.

What a stupid question. Caught in the fire just meant dead. "Stop! We don't need a bunch of speculation! It's possible these kids are just hanging out with friends somewhere in town. That's why we need full parent accountability of all children, and if anyone has seen or thinks they have seen any of these kids anywhere, or heard about where they are, please contact the sheriff's office at once."

"What about air assets?" another reporter asked. "Could aerial reconnaissance be deployed to search for the missing kids?"

"That's one of the biggest problems with this effort. I'm told winds are too great to safely operate aircraft."

A reporter in the middle of the group stood up. "I understand the county has some infrared scanning technology. Might that be used to scan through the smoke in the search for the children?"

This was the first time Chief Panetti wanted to punch a reporter in the middle of a briefing. But the guy was way back in the middle of the group. At least a few people groaned at the man's stupidity. "Yes, we have some helicopter-mounted infrared equipment. But the first problem is, as I've said, the winds are too strong for us to safely operate aircraft. The second problem, and this is kind of a big one, is that the IR equipment is scanning for heat, and yeah, any people under all that smoke will be emitting natural body heat. The other thing that's going to be putting out heat would be fire. It's gonna be real hard to isolate people at just shy of one hundred degrees when the entire area is burning at well over a thousand degrees."

The reporter's face flashed as red as a fire, and he sat back down.

"I think that's a good place to wrap this up. Thank you for your questions and especially for helping to get the word out about the missing young people. More information will be forthcoming on our website and Facebook page. URLs are written on the marker board over in the corner. Thank you. And to everybody out there, working on this crisis, good luck."

Maria Sanchez had been enjoying three weeks of nearly complete solitude in her friend's cabin. The internet was practically nonexistent there, but that was good. She'd needed to be free of distractions to finish her novel before the deadline. But then she'd seen smoke. The smoke got worse. Her friend had warned there might be a lot of smoke in late-summer Idaho. But then she'd glanced up from her writing to peek out the window and it had looked like a light snowfall. In August? It took a moment for her brain to put it together. Back in New York, she'd never had to worry about wildfires. These were ashes. There was a fire, a big one, and close.

She'd called her friend to ask what to do. *I'm sorry. All circuits are busy at this time. Please try your call again later. This is a recording.* A recording? Oh really? As if she couldn't tell. She tried again at once. Same message. She switched on the TV. Her friend had explained there was no cable or satellite. This thing was connected by a long wire to a digital antenna mounted a hundred feet up a tree clear on top of the mountain behind the cabin. She found the news, and it was all bad. "Oh no," she whispered. Almost without conscious thought, she grabbed her laptop with her manuscript and her flash-drive manuscript backup. She stuffed that, along with all her clothes, into her suitcase. All packed, she paced the small living room. Then she saw, on the screen, the words *evacuation order.* She was pretty sure the highlighted area of the on-screen map included her location. If not, it was close enough.

"*Highway 95 has been added to the list of roads closed to all but emergency vehicles and evacuation traffic,*" said a woman on the news. "*And now we have a report of a possible missing-children situation. Eight preteens, residents of McCall, have been reported miss—*"

She shut off the TV. Turned off the lights. Was there anything else she should do? Leave a note? Should she lock up? She decided against that. If some other terrified soul, fleeing the fire, needed a place to—what?—get some food or water or something, she wouldn't make them break in. If police or fire rescue came through and wanted to check for people, she'd make it easy for them. That gave her an idea, and she quickly taped a note to the door. *Maria Sanchez was staying in Ted Carrington's cabin. Evacuating to McCall. Nobody in this cabin.*

Then she lugged the heavy suitcase out to her little Prius, climbed in, and sped down the driveway. Even though it was still several hours before sunset, the sky was growing dark. Could the smoke really block out the light like that? How dark would it get? Turning south onto Highway 95, she pushed down on the gas. The speed limit was sixty miles per hour. Who cared about petty laws at a time like this? She would have happily gunned it up over a hundred, but the road was curvy, and she especially had to slow down for the rough road construction zone. Up ahead, smoke seemed to be rising from both sides of the highway.

It grew dark enough for her to need her headlights. She screamed a little as she rounded a curve and saw bright fire on the steep hillside to her left, hot sparks tracing through the dark toward the fire spreading out through a small clearing to the right.

Flash of taillights. She screamed again and hit the brakes. Ahead, a line of cars at a standstill. "Come on! Go!" she screamed. But nothing was moving. She turned on the air conditioner, as much to try to filter the smoke as to cool the air inside the car, but the fire was close to the road. She could feel the heat coming off the window beside her.

The world had descended into a nightmare darkness. Blackness all around, save for bright waves of fire up above on the slopes on both sides of the road. Sparks blew in the fierce wind above her, so that she was trapped in a tunnel of fire. About five yards ahead, a massive tree, coated in flames, slowly leaned toward the highway. People scrambled from the cars below and, with towels or other clothes wrapped around their heads, ran desperately away as the tree came crashing down over the road, smashing two cars, both of which burst into flames in seconds. A tree and two wrecked cars. The road to McCall was blocked.

Fleeing people slapped on the doors of the cars behind their destroyed vehicles. One car door opened to let one person in, but most of the cars must have been full. Finally some desperate stranded people reached her car, pounding on the windows and the roof. "Get in!" Maria shouted. They kept knocking. She remembered the locks, and hit the unlock button. In the next instant, three strangers squeezed into the backseat, and someone else flopped down in the passenger seat next to her.

"We gotta turn around!" said one of the newcomers. The people in back were mumbling about their totaled car, how much of their stuff was destroyed in the trunk.

Maria shifted into reverse and backed up, but hit the front bumper of the pickup behind her, whose driver honked. Everybody around her had the same idea. They were all trying to work the three-point—or ten-point—turn they'd need to head in the opposite direction.

"It's so hot out there," said someone from the back.

"Smokier here in the car," said another.

Someone screamed. Checking the rearview mirror, Maria quickly figured out what was wrong. Behind the column of desperately fleeing cars, another enormous burning tree fell over the road. They were trapped.

These strangers, these desperate people, as terrified as Maria, had climbed into her car for shelter, as a last-chance transport to safety. But more and more it looked as though they were all stuck out on the dark highway with the fire closing in.

"What do we do?" The girl who had screamed was starting to hyperventilate.

A horn sounded, loud enough to be heard over the other cars, pickups, and SUVs honking in panic. "Wait, wait, quiet!" Maria said. The horn sounded again. One of those loud air horns from a big semi truck.

The guy in her passenger seat pointed ahead. "Look!"

A semi hauling a flatbed trailer had backed up to the fallen tree in front of them. A man, maybe its driver, waved his arms over his head and pointed at the river beside the highway. It didn't take long for the first of the stranded travelers to figure it out. A mother led two crying children off the road to wade through the river, around the burning tree in front of them, and up to the truck. The driver helped them into his cab as Maria and the other stranded travelers stampeded to bypass the roadblock and catch a ride on the flatbed. When they were all aboard, and the semi honked and then rolled ahead toward McCall, Maria let out a relieved sigh, clutching her manuscript backup flash drive, grateful to be alive.

CHAPTER 12

YUMI HAD LED THE GROUP TO HAZARD CREEK EASILY enough. Well, it wasn't easy, but it was simple compared to trying to climb up the mountain or get over that giant crack that had nearly killed Annette.

Their current problem was so obvious, so horrible, that none of them had to mention it out loud. They'd all sunk into a quiet terror. So far, they had run from a front of fire, a scary wall of flame creeping up on them. But the winds had picked up, and shifted. And at least two separate fires had merged. Sparks had flown. The fire had jumped. Faster than anyone could have imagined, there were fires spread out on all sides now, and the thick smoke swirling in blacked out the sun, until day became night.

Kelton handed Yumi a flashlight. It helped a little bit, but they had to stay close to spot obstacles at the same time. There was really no point in Yumi leading the way anymore. She'd put away the map and compass. There was no more navigation. All they had left to do was follow this creek to Highway 95.

If they could make it there before the fire closed in. They all simply kept going. Running when they could, or moving along at a fast walk or scramble over rocks, under low branches. Everyone, including Yumi, tripped or fell a bunch of times.

"Where are the animals?" McKenzie asked. "We haven't seen one deer or raccoon running from all this. They just going to stay and burn?"

"Oh, I hope not," Morgan said.

Hunter coughed. "Animals—" He coughed again. The smoke was thick all around them. "Like deer? They can smell all this smoke from miles away. They can hear the fire crackling. They just take off. Fire crews almost never see dead burned animals. The animals are too smart to get caught up in . . ."

Yumi was glad when he shut up.

Annette moved up beside her. "We aren't going to make it, are we?"

A tree higher up on the slope to their left seemed to explode with fire. It cast enough light to help them see the way forward, and it sent a shower of sparks, like angry fireflies, down all around them.

"Ow!" Mason shouted. "Look out! Those things hurt! Right on the back of my neck!"

Hunter shouted too. Then Morgan.

"What about the creek?" McKenzie asked. "Maybe we could swim the rest of the way? The sparks can't go through water, right?"

"Mason? What do you think?" Yumi asked. He had become

the fire marshal of the group. She was pretty sure he hated the job.

Yumi glanced back at Mason, the orange firelight reflecting on his sweaty grimy face. There were tear tracks through the dust on his cheeks, either from fearful crying or from smoke irritation. Yumi probably looked the same. Mason frowned. "Maybe if the creek was higher. But it's real shallow in a lot of places. We'd be crawling or tripping over all the rocks in the creek bed. I think we'll move faster on land."

Nobody argued with him. They must have been too tired or too scared. And anyway what Mason said made a lot of sense. The sound was intense and getting louder. Yumi would have thought the flames would be silent, with just the crackling of burning wood, or maybe the loud crash of a falling tree. But the fire wasn't silent, and it didn't simply hiss. The dark woods all around them roared with an inhuman monstrous sound. In the early, unnatural dark, it sounded like ghosts, like monsters, or as if the entire earth shook with fury at them. As though the forest were punishing them for their intrusion, for trying to take its fish. The fire howled and screamed.

Rather than a solid wave of fire, the blaze burned in clusters, so that in the black bottom of the dark creek valley they stumbled on through a tunnel of flame. Trees and bushes ignited, crackling and whistling high up on the mountains on either side and at different elevations. Hot sparks blew fiercely above them.

Yumi was glad for the white spot of light from the flashlight.

It gave her and, she hoped, everyone else in her group a target, a direction. The flashlight fired a beacon that beckoned them forward. *Here! Go this way! Follow me, and do not be distracted by all the other burning lights here in the dark.*

"It's my fault," Annette said. She was speaking a little louder than she might have done to be heard over the roar of the flames. "My idea to go out to the woods fishing."

Yumi felt sorry for her friend. Guilt was hard. But Yumi had plenty of her own. Maybe if she had found a more direct route they could have stayed ahead of the fire. It was bad enough with the fire closing in all around them, and her aching body begged for rest after the many hard miles they'd charged through the woods. Annette was one of the best people Yumi had ever known. Yumi wanted to be a good friend. But she didn't need Annette's self-torture right now.

"If I had hurried over that log across that ravine," Annette said. "That wasted so much time."

"Enough!" Yumi said. "I get it. But there's plenty of blame to go around. If Morgan hadn't frozen up while she crossed the log. If I had a found a better route. If we'd all walked faster. If we hadn't spent so much time at the cabin. If we hadn't all wasted so much"—Yumi cursed—"time arguing over the stupid war. We're all bad. But unless you've got a time machine to go back to fix things, just . . ." She could see Annette's hurt expression in the dim firelight. "It's not going to help us, Ann. OK? We get home, we'll have a sleepover sometime and we can talk all about it then."

Yumi stopped for a moment and turned her head away from a shower of sparks falling before her.

"I'm sorry," Annette said.

"I'm sorry too," McKenzie said. Yumi sighed, but McKenzie continued. "I mean it. Because I, like, take the blame. All of this is looking like . . . well, it's bad, and it makes so much of what we've been arguing about, what I myself have been arguing about, seem so stupid now, OK?"

"A lot of that was my fault," Swann cut in.

McKenzie didn't say anything right away, and Yumi worried the peace would collapse right there. "Annette, you were apologizing for getting everybody into this, but you didn't invite me to Painted Pond. I overheard you and we went for it. So I got Morgan and Mason into this. But when we were trapped up there on top of the mountain, Annette, that was so cool how you got that hatchet out and started chopping. It took all of us together to build that bridge.

"So, yeah. In, like, the time we have left," McKenzie said jokingly, "let's be friends."

She held out an offer for a fist bump, even as a tree in the distance behind her erupted in a towering inferno. Swann touched her fist to McKenzie's. Morgan joined in. Yumi held up her fist from a distance.

But Annette offered her fist slowly, not even looking at the others. "Maybe . . . we have more time than we thought."

What was Annette talking about? Yumi followed her gaze. "What is it?"

"Look! What's that?" Annette pointed far ahead of them toward a white light.

"A brighter fire?" Mason said. "Something burning hotter?"

"No!" Annette said. "Come on. Ahead of us, down there. That's not fire. Right?"

The light moved, first to their right, then stopping, before moving back to the left. And when it moved back to the left, it must have cleared a tree, because now they could see two white lights.

"Headlights!" Yumi shouted. "It's a car or something!"

"The road?" Morgan called.

"Or *a* road!" Yumi yelled. "Come on! Let's go! There's someone there who could give us a ride!" She led the charge ahead, flicking the flashlight on and off. That vehicle was still a long way away. If she could signal to the driver, they might stop for them.

It was as if a new energy had flared up in all of them just as fast as many of the trees were igniting. They ran or walked as quickly as they could, all of them talking about how the lights could mean safety at last. Some of them even laughed.

Then the distant lights vanished. Yumi let out a sigh and wanted to collapse on the ground and give up.

"It's OK," Annette said. "The lights had to come from a road up there somewhere. Roads lead to roads. Just keep going."

Yumi had no idea how Annette could remain so hopeful, but she was glad she did. The group moved on, an agony of sore feet, aching muscles, and more and more small painful burns from hot flying ashes. Finally, they emerged from the heavier tree cover, and then, as if by a miracle, Yumi's flashlight shined upon something that shined back. A Highway 95 road sign!

"Hey!" Yumi shouted. "This is it! This is the road!" She laughed. "We made it!"

The whole group cheered as they scrambled up onto the pavement, their shoes crunching on more burned out cinders there.

Swann and Kelton hugged. Hunter threw his arms around Annette. Mason picked Yumi up in a big bear hug and swung her around, laughing. Morgan and McKenzie danced.

"You did it, Yumi!" Annette said. "You brought us through."

"Wait a minute," Yumi said. Something was wrong. They weren't thinking about this right. "Wait a minute! Put me down! Hey!"

She felt bad for killing the party, but what she had to say couldn't wait. "This isn't right. It's still dark as night." She pulled out her phone. It was only seven. There were hours of daylight left. They'd been so excited about reaching the highway that none of them had been paying attention. "The fire's spread a lot farther than we thought." The Little Salmon River ran along to the west of the highway, and beyond that, more burning woods. "The fire's jumped the river."

"Does that mean the road's cut off?" Morgan asked. "Please tell me we didn't come all this way for nothing."

"Maybe we should just get in the river," Annette said. "The fire can't possibly burn through water."

"I wish that could work," Mason said. "It would be sweet

to simply float south to safety in New Meadows. But the Little Salmon River flows north."

"There was a car!" McKenzie said. "Or a truck or something. Some people are still driving this road. Or trying to. Let's follow the road south, at least for as long as we can. The river runs along by the side of the road most of the way. We can jump in the water as a last resort, but in the meantime, let's head toward New Meadows and get help."

McKenzie was right, and Yumi was happy when the others quickly agreed. They paused only long enough for Hunter to use his water filter to pump clean water from the river, filling their CamelBaks.

"Come on, Higgins!" Yumi shouted. "You're taking forever! We gotta go!" She hated yelling at Hunter, but the fire was closing in.

"Just fill them with river water," said Kelton. "What's the difference?"

Hunter kept pumping. "The difference is a zillion microscopic organisms in the water."

"Plus ash," said Mason.

"You want to drink all that?" Hunter asked. "Get sick and poop your guts out for a week? Go ahead. Or wait a second, and this filter pump will take out the bad stuff. Make it safe to drink."

"Fine," Yumi said. "But that's enough. Let's go!"

Hunter packed up his pump, and with everyone chugging desperately needed fresh and crisp clear cool water, the group returned to the highway and headed south. After so long in the woods, being on the pavement felt like a dream. They didn't have to worry nearly so much about tripping, and without even talking about it, they soon sped into a light jog. It made no sense trying to run as fast as they could when they still had miles to go.

But soon enough the road rounded a corner and headed toward heartbreak again. Just past a road construction area, the highway was jammed with broken vehicles that had been on a last-chance desperate drive. A mix of six cars and trucks had been reduced to a burning roadblock. Fire roared in the trees and shrubs between the pavement and the river.

"Oh no," Annette said. She leaned forward, peering into the mess before them. "It's hard to tell, but it looks like the vehicles are all empty. I mean, I don't see any . . . you know."

Yumi felt like someone had punched her in the chest. This was it. What could they do now? What was left? Hiding in the river? She staggered back, off the road onto the gravel shoulder area that had been expanded for the construction. She felt dizzy, and leaned against the muddy track of a piece of heavy equipment. She coughed against the smoke.

"What do we do? What do we do?" Morgan asked. "We can't get past those burning cars, those trees! If the cars are stuck, so are we!"

McKenzie sat down on the ground and hung her head. Annette paced, shoulders slumped. Hunter stepped up to Yumi's side. Mason stood before her.

"Hey, you OK, Yumi?" Mason asked. "You don't look so good."

"He means, you look worse than you have since this all started," Hunter said.

"What are we going to do?" Yumi whispered, more like a wheeze. She could hardly breathe. "I'm out of ideas. I got nothing."

"Hey, Hunter." Annette's puffy hair fluttered in the breeze. "Your grandpa owns a road construction company, right?"

"What does that have to do with anything?" Yumi asked.

Hunter motioned around the job site. "He didn't get this contract, though. His company is working near Boise."

"But he has big things like this?" Annette pointed at the machine behind Yumi.

"Bulldozers?" Hunter said. "Sure. He has a few of them. Why?"

"Ever drive one?" Annette asked.

Yumi squeezed her eyes tightly shut and then opened them again, taking a deep breath and rising to her feet. "No way. Grandpa wouldn't let either of us drive a bulldozer."

"These things cost, like, a quarter of a million dollars new," Hunter explained. "But we've both driven Grandpa's skid steer. That's a big track-wheeled machine."

Yumi smiled. She looked from the full-sized bulldozer to the burned-cars roadblock. "Higgins, are you thinking what I'm thinking?"

"If what you're thinking is really dumb, then yes, I am," Hunter said.

McKenzie stood up. "What? What does that mean?"

Yumi pointed around the construction site. "A couple of lunch boxes scattered around. Some tools. "This bulldozer is parked totally randomly. The construction guys didn't quit for the day. They evacuated in a panic. Which means . . ." She exchanged a smile with Hunter before they both scrambled up the machine's steps to the cab. Yumi rushed inside and slid into the seat first. "Bingo! Keys!"

Hunter pointed at the controls. "You want me to—"

"I got it!" Yumi said. "Here, hold this!" She handed Hunter the flashlight and he shined it on the controls. "OK, so turns out this is a lot different than Grandpa's skid steer. But that's not going to stop me. Grandpa actually showed me all this on his bulldozer once." It was kind of a lot to remember. She hoped she'd get it right. Yumi turned the key partway, waiting for the annoying buzz sound to stop. When it did, she turned the key the rest of the way and the engine roared to life. Maybe it was her imagination, but she thought she could smell that horrible stench of diesel fumes, even over the smoke all around them.

Yumi stood up from her seat and leaned out the window. "All right!" She shouted at her friends. "This has been the most messed-up fishing trip of my life. I'm tired from walking. Tired of these stupid little embers burning me. And most of all, I'm tired of running away, in fear for my life. I say we go home. Climb in, and let's go bust open the road!"

She worried about all of them fitting in the cab. The seat was designed for a big tough construction-worker type of man, so seventh-graders fit a little better. Hunter and Yumi sat in the seat. There was a little dead space behind the seat and on either side. Annette sat on Hunter's lap. McKenzie and Morgan climbed up and squeezed in back. Swann and Kelton curled up in the little space to either side of the seat. It was tight. A clown car of nightmares. Mason gripped the handle by the door and stood on the small platform outside the cab.

"I'll duck inside if the fire gets to be too much," Mason said.

"There's not even a steering wheel," Annette said. "Yumi, how are you going to drive this thing?"

Yumi gripped the drive lever. "It's all right here. Grandpa talked me though it once, just showing Higgins and me when we asked him the same question."

Hunter pointed at the smaller of the two floor pedals, the one on the right. "So that's throttle. Remember it's the opposite of a regular gas pedal. It'll kill power the more you push on it."

"That's stupid," Kelton said. "Why would they make it like that?"

Yumi shrugged. "Don't know. Don't care." She grabbed the smaller lever on her right. The engine was in neutral. This lever couldn't hurt anything. "I think . . ." She pulled the lever back, the machine noise changed, and the dozer blade lifted off the ground. "Bingo! Blade control." She raised the giant steel blade in front of them about a foot off the ground. "Can't have that dragging everywhere." A burning tree branch fell right over the steel arms that held the blade.

"Let's go already, Yumi!" McKenzie shouted.

Yumi exchanged a look with Hunter. He nodded. "You remember all this, Cousin. You were paying a lot more attention to Grandpa's demonstration."

"Sure," Yumi said. "I got this." *No. I do not got this.*

Yumi twisted the handle on the drive lever from neutral to forward and the bulldozer jumped ahead fast. Mason shouted, almost falling off his platform. McKenzie hit her head on the window.

Yumi stomped the throttle control pedal to the floor, dropping them back to an idle. "Sorry!" She tried again, easing the throttle pedal up to give the machine more power, and they moved ahead. She pushed the drive lever forward a little to turn left. She did not have to push it much. The machine turned faster than she expected. Then she straightened their course and let up the throttle pedal to power up and move onto the road. Pulling the drive lever back turned them to the right and she lined up the machine with the center of the highway.

Annette bounced up and down. "So we're just going to smash right through the cars?"

Yumi shrugged. Was she going to get in trouble for this? There were laws against crushing other people's cars. Did the laws change in the middle of a forest fire? "Ah, they're toast anyway."

"Yeah!" Kelton clapped his hands. He was curled up in a little ball in the tiny side space to Yumi's right, but he was giddy. "Let's smash it up! Go, Yumi! Go! It's like the snowmobile jump at Stone Cold Gap. There's no doing this halfway. Full power!"

Kelton was annoying at times, but a good guy, and he was absolutely right about this.

"Everybody hold on!" Yumi let the throttle pedal come all the way up and the big Cat bulldozer lurched ahead, vibrating and roaring down the middle of Highway 95.

Mason ducked inside the cab and braced himself as they neared the closest burning tree. "Yeah!" He laughed. "Coming through!"

The dozer rattled fast, closer and closer to the fiery mess ahead. Twelve feet. Eight. Five. Two. The bulldozer smashed the first tree, slamming it into the cars, and while Yumi thought the impact would throw them all ahead, she was surprised at how easily the dozer crushed the tree and cars aside. First the clump of disabled cars smashed and skidded along in front of them. Then they collided with the next car, and one of the first crashed cars was pushed off the blade to the side. Flames rose up over the front of the blade as they hit the second tree, pushing it and two burning cars down the highway.

"What are we going to do?" Annette asked. "Just push this flaming pile all the way back to McCall? We could spread so much fire."

"Fine, then." Yumi pulled the drive lever handle to turn the bulldozer right. She pushed the burning cars and tree into a steaming pile in the river. Backing up in the bulldozer was tricky. The machine kept wanting to back the opposite direction she'd intended. Eventually, she gave up, put it in forward, and rolled ahead.

The group cheered when Yumi finally set them full-throttle down the middle of the open road. McKenzie even hugged her. Kelton patted her shoulder. Morgan wiped her teary eyes, and Yumi had to admit, she understood how the girl felt.

"Higgins, take the drive lever." Yumi grabbed her phone. Thirty percent battery would be enough. She tapped out a text to her mom, dad, and to 911. First she tapped out all of their names. Then a simple message: *We are alive*. She tapped send, and hoped they would make it close enough to connect to the cellular network soon.

Highway 95 is far from a big, straight, four lane interstate highway. The narrow road winds back and forth with the river, so that Yumi had to press down the throttle pedal to ease off the power as she negotiated the turns. It wasn't easy. Grandpa was a crack shot on equipment like this. Yumi almost dumped them off the road into the river more than once. But she wouldn't stop. She would never stop.

TOMOKO HIGGINS WOULDN'T STOP PACING. SHE'D TRIED SITTING
in the command center tent, but it was like an oven in there and
loud from the tent fluttering in the wind. She paced the parking
lot, sure she was feeling what Yumi must have felt—must be
feeling—if she really was somewhere out there in those burning
woods. Every few trips back and forth across the parking lot she'd
step close to her husband Rick and he'd squeeze her close, a crime
in this heat, but still comforting, at least for a short time. She
simply had to keep moving. She couldn't explain it.

In contrast, Rick stood statue-still, at his brother David's side.
"I hate this," Rick said quietly to his brother. "It was so much
easier back in the war, even on our darkest day. At least then we
could fight back. Now we're just so . . ."

"Helpless," David agreed. He let out a little sad laugh. "This
is twice this year Hunter's done this to us. I swear, I'll never let
him out in the woods again. If we ever see—" He choked up.
Rick patted his back. Tomoko noted Rick didn't try to encourage
his brother, didn't say that he was sure the kids were OK, that of
course they'd see Hunter again. And Yumi.

Fighting a forest fire was like doing battle against a living thing.
That's part of the reason why Rob Endsen and a lot of the men he
worked with loved the job so much. They'd be out there, hacking
away at bushes or trees with chain saws, axes, or rakes, taking
down a fire's fuel. Or, as now, fighting hard to prevent the fire
from jumping their lines and moving south or west. They'd lost
control of too much of Highway 95. They were determined not to

lose any more. If the fire advanced much farther, they were going to have to start evacuating sections of the town of New Meadows and maybe even McCall. The people back there were already on evacuation standby alert, terrified, praying for the success of the firefighting effort. Rob felt the energy of their prayers as he held a big fire hose, blasting a thick clump of bushes at the base of a pine with all the water he could. About ten minutes ago, the wind had finally shifted back north and was at last dying down, giving them a chance. He kept the water flowing. He wasn't going to extinguish this part of the fire. His goal was to let it consume that big bunch of fuel, but to hold the fire there, washing down the sparks to reduce the odds of this thing spreading farther.

"Come on, you hot monster!" Rob cursed. "Settle down, now," he said to the flames. "You will not take New Meadows and you darn sure won't take McCall!"

A shout, a cheer, went up from the guys behind him. Rob risked a glance back and quickly spotted what had them so excited. A low-flying twin-engine Lockheed P-2 Neptune airplane soared in over the west side of the highway. It dropped its pink fire retardant chemical spray.

"Yeah!" Rob joined the cheer.

Even with his entire front side painfully hot, he advanced, spraying that water into the burning grove before him, listening to the fire's roar, the hiss of steam as his water cooked off almost instantly. He laughed. The flames were backing down. His attack here was working. He might be starting to push back the fire.

A few minutes later he heard the rest of the men cheering

again. He turned and saw some shaking their fists in the air. Then he heard the buzz, that beautiful engine sound, as a plane came in to drop water to help the ground fight. In the distance on the first plane's flight path was a second plane. The aircraft would be coming in from all over! With the daylight they had left, they'd dig in and make progress fighting this fire.

What would Tomoko do if she lost her baby out there? How could she go on? She'd have to close her store. She couldn't keep hosting wine tastings and live music to happy tourists when she herself was dead inside. She ran her fingers through her hair. What did any of this matter? Nothing mattered but that Yumi be safe. "Please," she whispered. "Oh, my sweet girl."

Her phone buzzed in her pocket. It was probably her mom calling from Japan for the tenth time, asking for updates. She had none, so she really didn't want to talk to her. But by force of habit, Tomoko already had her phone in hand. It was a text.

We are alive.

Tomoko screamed. She rubbed her eyes, rechecked the message, and screamed again.

Rob Endsen loved this part of battling a blaze, when the energy had changed and they were finally starting to make some progress. It reminded him of some great come-from-behind football games in high school. When the team came together and the momentum shifted and victory was in sight. This was a nightmare fire, the worst he'd ever seen, but with air support finally joining in and the winds dying down a little, he and the guys were more excited to finally start hitting back.

From the distance, from back in the thick smoke, came a low rumble. At first he thought it was another aircraft. But the noise was too deep. And moments later, the ground shook. Up the road the smoke shifted. And was that—it was! A light. "Car coming through!" he shouted to the others. The guys needed to be aware someone was coming in, to make sure they didn't accidentally direct a hose over there and nail some poor guy's windshield with a high-pressure blast of water.

A bulldozer emerged from the smoke. A kid stood on the step outside the cab, smiling and waving, doing a little dance. Rob shook his head. He'd seen a lot of unbelievable sights in his time fighting fires, but a group of kids driving themselves to safety in a giant scorched bulldozer might have been the craziest he'd seen so far.

What were they supposed to do? Those kids were way beyond the firefighting line and therefore in trouble. He ought to go try to rescue them. But they were coming in at about five miles per hour and would clear the line very soon. Anyway, he couldn't leave his position, and it didn't look like the kids were interested in stopping. No way Rob was going to stop that machine. Who knew how far they'd already driven the dozer? Might as well let them bring it in.

As the bulldozer crossed their lines, ambulances and police vehicles rolled in from McCall and New Meadows. Seconds later, police, EMTs, and a bunch of excited civilians climbed out of the vehicles, surrounding the dozer, which had finally come to a stop, its engine shutting down.

Rob had to pay attention to the fire in front of him, so he turned away, but even over the roar of the fire and the shouts of the men on his crew communicating with one another, he could still hear, behind him, the cries, laughter, cheers, and warm greetings of a very happy reunion.

CHAPTER 13

THE WEIRDEST PART OF FINALLY DRIVING TO SAFETY, apart from the hard-to-believe fact that they hadn't all died, was the nearly instant transformation of the world around them. One moment they were rattling down the road in a dark-as-night smoke-and-fire nightmare, and the next they'd cleared the smoke and emerged into the light of a late summer evening.

Annette squeezed Yumi's shoulder. "You did it! You brought us to safety!" The cab was full of cheering, laughter, and high fives.

As police cars and ambulances rolled up to meet them, Yumi stopped the dozer and shut off the engine.

Sometime on the bulldozer ride back to McCall, all their phones had finally connected, and were lit up with missed call and text notifications. Thanks to Yumi's forward-thinking text message, people back home soon knew they were alive. They'd wasted no time rushing to meet them.

So. Many. Hugs.

When the time finally came for Annette to sit down to write the school newspaper article about the fiery fishing trip she and her friends had survived, she'd try one of those ending-first openings, describing their bulldozer ride to safety and then the sea of hugs that awaited all of them as soon as they'd climbed down from the machine. It was incredible. Annette supposed she'd eventually be in trouble for borrowing the John Deere Gator and getting it destroyed, but for the moment she enjoyed being squeezed between her mom and dad.

"Annette! Oh, my sweet girl!" Mom kept saying it. Again and again. Then Dad joined in. He'd nearly destroyed the car on the fastest drive he'd ever made up from Boise. Even Dakota, Gabe, Kyle, and Janelle seemed excited to see her. It was funny. Annette had gone out to the woods seeking adventure, and then found too much. For years, she'd longed for real attention from her family, and especially from Mom and Dad. Now she had almost more than she could handle.

Then came questions from the police, paramedics, and firefighters. Yumi was extra-worried about the bulldozer. "I was only borrowing it," she tried to explain. "But I guess you police hear that from every thief you've ever caught."

But the owner of the bulldozer showed up. "Don't worry about it, miss," he said. "I'm just glad you kids are safe, glad my machine could help. And no damage done. Well, hardly any. You brought it in safely when otherwise it might have been all burned up."

After a very long day when all the people in her group had plenty of time to talk to one another, once they were back they didn't have a chance to talk among themselves at all. The questions, medical checkups, and "I love you so much" repetitions from parents kept coming. Everyone else must have been about as overwhelmed by it all as Annette, because her whole group exchanged looks and laughed. All she wanted to do was go home, shower, maybe eat something besides baked beans, chocolate pudding, and crackers, and then get some sleep. McKenzie yawned, and, catching Annette's attention, rolled her eyes like, *Can you believe all this?*

Of course, among the parents were Hunter's and Yumi's. Yumi's dad was nice, but he was a big guy, and Annette had always suspected, if he were really mad, he could be scary. He turned really scary that night, after the newspeople showed up. Annette usually respected reporters. She wanted so badly to be one of them. A real one. But that evening, after everything they'd been through, she did not want to deal with a fresh round of questions.

Staff Sergeant Rick Higgins came to the rescue. "Thanks for your interest." His voice boomed over the noise from the reporters. "But our kids are tired, and they just want to go home and get some rest. You can get in touch with us through the sheriff's office later."

And that was it. The sheriff and two of his deputies cleared the way for them all to get to their parents' cars, and minutes later Annette was safe at home. After a shower and her favorite supper—Mom's spaghetti—she was finally able to lay her aching body down in her soft safe bed, the afterimage of the fire in the smoky darkness flickering behind her eyelids and into her dreams.

Two weeks later, the whole fishing trip group, including McKenzie, Morgan, and Mason now, met at Swann's house. Annette had never been in such an amazing home before. It was right on the lake, with a beautiful view after two days of rain last week had finally helped put out the last of the fires and cleaned the air a little. Annette had told herself over and over to be cool. She hoped she appeared normal on the outside, but greeting them all in the big high-ceilinged dining room were Swann's parents, Swann's father without all the vampire makeup from the *Snowtastrophe* movies and her mother who had been so much fun to watch in the Hallmark movie *Back to the Hometown Christmas*. They were right there in front of her. Real people. She was in *their* house.

"Don't mind us," said Swann's mother. She gestured in a neat flowing summer dress toward a counter in the kitchen covered in all kinds of snacks and drinks. Pretzels, pizza, a cheese board, chips, candy, and more, plus big metal tubs full of ice and soda. "Help yourselves. You don't have to ask. We got it for you. We're just so happy you all made it home safe from that fire."

Minutes later, each carrying his or her own tray of treats, they followed Swann through her big house and up a spiral staircase to the glorious tower-top library. Under a cone ceiling, from which a big basket swing hung by a rope, and surrounded by tall bookshelves interrupted only by four equidistant windows offering spectacular views of the lake and the woods, the group met.

"I know this is crazy or may seem dumb," Swann said, holding up a can of Coke. "But I'm glad everyone's here. It's a nice chance to get together after everything that happened. We kind of worked things out together in the burning woods, but then all we had time for was a simple fist bump, so I figured we should have a party. To celebrate making it through, thanks to everyone. Here's to the survivors." People held their drinks up. Swann sighed. "You're supposed to repeat, 'The survivors.'"

"There's Swann, always so bossy," McKenzie said, but everybody could tell she was joking. They laughed and echoed, "The survivors."

McKenzie played some music from her phone and everyone dug into their snacks. They talked about school, about the sports seasons that had begun. And at last, now that the danger was past, they were able to laugh about some of the misadventures they'd endured.

In the time since the ordeal, Annette had tried to write about it. She'd searched the internet for a quotation to use for a great opening, but nothing she'd found seemed right.

"I am the author of my own quotations," she'd finally written in her notebook.

She was grateful for the conversation about how they'd gone fishing in fire. It helped her realize something important about her writing. She had gone into the woods to live her own story, after all. But the words wouldn't come. She couldn't get them right. And she realized, now that she was reunited with the group, with her friends, that she had failed to capture, on paper, the truth of that fiery day because the story was not hers alone. It belonged to all of them together.

Annette stepped up to Hunter, who was looking out a window upon the lake and the forest. "You OK?" she asked him. He was so quiet, gazing at the world so intently. After a moment he looked at her and smiled. She loved that smile.

"I'm great, thanks to you." he said. "Just thinking how it will be deer-hunting season soon."

She moved closer to him and they held hands. "How will you top last year?"

"I'll start by bringing in a deer instead of a wolf." He laughed, but then grew serious. "And I'll invite you to come along."

McKenzie must have said something really funny across the library by the desk. Swann and Morgan laughed.

Yumi stepped up to them, watching them carefully. "So you two . . ."

"Yep," Hunter said.

"About time," Yumi said.

Annette nodded toward Mason, who pretended to be looking over Swann's books, but kept sneaking glances at Yumi. "And you two?"

Yumi smiled and shrugged. "We'll see. He invited me to go fishing with him and his dad on their boat next weekend. I said yes."

Hunter exchanged a glance with Annette. "But you're not that big into fishing."

"Know what, Higgins?" Yumi gave him a light tap-punch to the shoulder. "It's growing on me."

Kelton approached, and Swann soon followed. Annette pointed out the window. "We had the close call with the wolf, the trouble up on Storm Mountain, and then this fire. Are we really going back out there?"

"Oh yeah." Yumi shrugged. "This is Idaho."

Hunter nodded. "There's so much adventure out there."

Annette looked around at her group of friends, and then turned her attention out to the great Idaho wilderness, which stretched away over mountains and valleys and rivers for millions of acres. She sighed and smiled. "We're just getting started."

ACKNOWLEDGMENTS

AND SO WE REACH THE END OF THE MCCALL MOUNTAIN series. I hope readers have enjoyed *Hunter's Choice*, *Racing Storm Mountain*, and *Fishing in Fire* as much as I have enjoyed writing them. It has been so fun sending these characters out on adventures. Thank you so much for reading. And for *Fishing in Fire* in particular, special thanks go:

Once again to the wonderful people of McCall, Idaho. I'm amazed at the town's beauty, and every time I visit, I have a great time. It's the perfect setting for books. What's not to love about McCall?

To Matt and Mason Bridges, the greatest fishing experts. Mason, I'm so glad I was the substitute teacher in your class that one day. Thank you both for the gift of your time and for your knowledge of fishing. Any fishing errors remaining in the book are all my fault.

To Pam Watts, Matthew Kirby, Jessica Denhart, and Jennifer Schmidt, all brilliant writers and wonderful friends.

Thank you for helping me in the difficult months following the betrayal of Afghanistan. Thank you very much for your patience with me. I owe you all more than I can ever repay.

To the Norton Young Readers family for all their help, with extra thanks to my editor, Simon Boughton, whose inspiration and guidance made this all possible. Thanks, Norton friends. This has been wonderful.

To my wonderful super-agent, Ammi-Joan Paquette, for connecting me with Mr. Boughton and Norton Young Readers. The McCall Mountain books wouldn't exist without you.

To my daughter, Verity, who was so patient and encouraging while I worked on all of these books. Thanks for helping me come up with Swann Siddiq's character. You were right. The story did need a princess.

To my wonderful wife, Amanda, whose total support in life, patience with me, and encouragement of my writing has meant everything, especially during the challenging times during which I wrote *Fishing in Fire*. Thank God for you. Amanda, you are my life.